FEEDING STRAWBERRIES TO PIGS

SHORT STORIES

by

Gerry Rose

Best wishes

Gerry

2010

ORIGINAL WRITING

Cover painting by Lesley Lauriston

ISBN: 978-1-907179-50-1

A CIP catalogue for this book is available from the National Library.

Published by ORIGINAL WRITING LTD, Ireland, 2010

Printed by CAHILLS PRINTERS LIMITED

Dedicated To Rory, Mammy and Daddy

Acknowledgements

Long may there be people who stand by you and with you in life and keep you going.

There were many dark and desperate days from August 2003 onwards and in no particular order here are the people who held me up and made life worth living:

My son Angus, Sue Clokey, Joanne Neil, Adrianne and Brian Jones, Rita and Godfrey (who have also been my editors) our dog Guinness, The Brandtzaeg family, the village of Cretingham, Victoria Sangster, Steven Hayes, Rory's friends and my late mother, Susanna.

Introduction

'Feeding strawberries to pigs'
'The people you see when you haven't got a gun'
'For every old sock, there's an old shoe'
'Be civil, but strange.'
'Nature shines through the eyes of a cat.'
'As delicate as bully, when he ate the dishcloth.'

I grew up with these sayings: my parents were Irish immigrants to England so I am the product of my Anglo-Irish upbringing. I live in a world that is in-between two cultures. I used to feel that I belonged nowhere. Now I realise that I have been enriched by these diverse influences and my obsession with these issues has informed my writing.

When I am in Ireland I feel there is a bond with the people and their outlook, but unfortunately for me, when I speak people think I must be English. Many Irish people cannot accept that I am Irish. I also recognise that a part of me is English, and this makes for an interesting creative mix.

These stories seek to show, what it has been like to grow up Irish in England. I have also attempted to explore what being Irish means.

I have also let my imagination wander rather a lot. I hope you enjoy them!

CONTENTS

EDUCATION, EDUCATION, EDUCATION

Old habits die hard, and even though Sister Margaret does not look like a nun, with her lack of a formal habit, I am reverent and polite. Yes Sister, no Sister. I am sitting in her office at Bethlehem house, a statue of Jesus is still exposing his bleeding organ for all to see. Some things never change.

'Doctor Clarke, I'm glad you could see me at such short notice, there are a few things I would like to discuss with you, regarding your mother's condition.'

I remember the bumper sticker that the Americans are rather fond of. *'Be nice to your children-remember they will choose your care home.'*

'Your mother can be, now how should I put this, difficult and rather profane.'

'You mean she swears?'

'Well yes, Doctor Clarke.'

I stifle a laugh, look serious and say, 'oh dear, that must be difficult for you Sister.'

'Yes and it feels as though your mother doesn't seem to like nuns, Doctor Clarke.'

'Yes Sister, I know.' Was all I could reply.

Essex 1966

There are two radios competing with each other in my

house. My big sister Angela has a transistor that spills out its tinny offerings of the latest hits. Football fever is gripping the nation and the best song on offer is 'World Cup Willy'. My parents' wireless in the kitchen is tuned to the Home Service. I am sitting in my brushed polyester dressing gown, eating toast, trying to prolong the time before I will have to leave for school. Everyone knows today is the day, but no one mentions it. Too much rests on today, my family's hopes, and the reputation of the entire Irish nation.

My mother has 'notions' she wants her family to be successful, to prove to those back home that leaving was the right decision, but so far things have not worked according to plan. My father picks up his sandwiches wrapped in the empty bread bag and looks at me. He pauses, and then says, 'Goodbye Philomena' and leaves. Mother looks at me and says, 'Sure why are you dawdling? Don't you know the clock races when it gets to eight.'

Angela thunders down the stairs carrying my little sister. Mother hands them their lunches and then suddenly all hell breaks loose.

'Holy Mary, Mother of God, what are you wearing?'

Mother gives Angela one of her filthy looks.

Angela has dressed Dolores and she is certainly a sight, I suppose you could describe it as tarty. I never understood at the time, why my mother called her last daughter Dolores and why Angela had sole care of our little sister.

When I arrived at school the atmosphere was so highly charged it was palpable. There were some that were nonchalant. The 11 plus results did not concern them, their futures were written on clocking-in cards, endless forms with obscure numbers or the never-ending factory conveyer belt or Woolworths. Others were cocky unable to contemplate any sort of failure. But many were like me and knew that this day would be forever etched on their memory. I am back there now, a day that is far more memorable than my wedding day.

The bell goes and we file into the hall where the Headmistress says we must wait to hear if our name is called. I am low in the alphabet. 'Karen Allway'. Of course, she is in group G like me. Who did those teachers think they were kidding, calling our groups G, B and F? They must have realised that we would work out quite quickly that the initials = Good, Bad and Fair. I stand frozen hardly able to breathe. I should be next. I hear 'Mary Parker' and think a mistake has been made. When Mrs Moss announces that the ten successful candidates are excused lessons that day and will be having a party, I feel like dying. At break time, I am crying as I press my face against the cool hall window watching my friends. I am a failure.

Mother weeps again when the letter arrives, a standard letter with the highly arrogant phrase- *is not deemed suitable for higher education.* She threw it into the fire, but I pulled it out and still have it, the words hurt more than flames ever could. All hope had gone. She looked at me with her face that had years of disappointments etched into the lines beside her down-turned mouth and said, 'We had such high hopes for you.'

My saving grace was that my mother knew how to play the game- 'Irish Catholic'. When the shock had subsided, she began her campaign. She started with distributing the brown carrier bags throughout the parish for the church Christmas bazaar donations. Then she moved on to embroidering tray cloths full of shamrocks, to sell on the linen stall. Having been seen to do what was required, she made an appointment to see the Reverend Mother to plead her case.

On the day of the appointment I prayed like never before, down on my knees in front of the picture of the Sacred Heart, a bottle of Lourdes water and a postcard of the dead President Kennedy for good measure. Mother arrived home graven faced; she had walked all the way in her good pair of shoes. She took off her blue coat with the fur collar and sat exhausted in the chair. I was watching 'Blue Peter' with Dolores, trying to memorise the things that Valerie Singleton said, because if I got into the Convent I was going to have to speak with a good English accent.

We waited in silence until dad got home. When we heard him wheeling his cycle up the side passage my heart leapt and my face burnt; I thought I would die from suspense. Dad came in and took his donkey jacket off, looking even hotter than I was; he had cycled hard, to be home quickly to hear the news.

'Well Nancy?' was all he could manage, mother started in a very Irish way that I was to find so infuriating in later life. She told every detail in its exact order. How she rang the big brass bell and an ancient nun bent over like a hairpin had opened the door and invited her in her broad Kerry accent, to sit in a room with lovely big heavy oak chairs and tables. How the Convent smelled of lavender furniture polish and had beautiful vases of flowers by every statue, how the Reverend Mother was 'upper bracket' English and spoke to her in haughty tones, but how the rest of the nuns were Irish. All we wanted to know was could I go, how much would it cost and how would we afford it? We eventually heard the words. 'Well she can go, but...' Time stood still, to have got so near but so far would destroy me.

I had been thinking about the uniform for weeks. I had dreamed I was wearing the navy skirt which had to lay a regulation four inches on the ground as you knelt. The red girdle that was worn tied around the waist. The navy and red striped tie. The blazer with the red badge with the swirly red S.M. and C. intertwined on the breast pocket. The soft navy felt hat and the straw boater in the summer worn with the royal blue shirtdress and white cotton gloves. The word 'but' lay heavy in the air. We waited for mother to continue.

'She will have to behave herself and work very hard. They could not have anyone who would let down the reputation of St Mary's Convent.' My mother gave my father a knowing look and they both lowered their heads. They looked embarrassed and guilty; I found this strange at the time.

Things changed in our family. My mother joined Angela at the shoe factory and father worked extra shifts. I learned that to be Irish was considered by some to be unacceptable, so I lost my accent quickly. My new accent upset others and I crossed the road to avoid gangs of disaffected English children, who attended schools that taught them envy and hate.

At school, girls called Helena, Verity and Felicity who lived in big houses with hand basins and televisions in their bedrooms, found me amusing. But their parents who knew where I lived were wary; they always asked what my father did for a living, I lied.

At school I learned that wealthy girls were allowed to stay in at lunchtimes, whilst poor girls were expected to stay outside and freeze. In my second hand uniform I was definitely a second class pupil.

I smile at Sister Margaret and say, 'It's a terrible disease Alzheimer's, but she is in the best possible place for her.'

I hand her a cheque for new altar cloths for their chapel and leave with a clear conscience. Happy that at last my mother no longer has to bow and scrape, and has the freedom of spirit to behave as she really wanted to all those years ago.

MICHAEL MURPHY'S LAW

Michael put his head out of the door and sniffed loudly, there was the distinct smell of spring, a sort of freshness that promises gentle warm days and a softness to the ground which a shower leaves behind. He was glad that winter was behind him, it had been a time of hibernation and the all pervading smell of hatred and death. Spring meant new beginnings, and with Easter early this year he felt as if he was crawling out from under a stone that had pinned him down for too long.

He felt a sudden urge to get out of the house that had bound him and take a walk. He stepped back inside to get his summer coat, it was still in the polythene bag from the dry cleaners and as he pulled the coat off its hanger, the hanger bent and snapped like a broken bone but he smiled to himself. He grabbed his straw hat and opened the front door a little, the stale odour of his house escaping like air from a balloon. As he stepped out he was knocked to the ground by a hooded teenager who was riding his bike on the pavement. Michael picked himself up and giggled. The sound was surprising, like a piece of music that he hadn't heard for a long time, yet knew so well. He used to giggle a lot as a child and was even known as 'the giggler' at school.

A sudden breeze blew his straw hat off and it went

dancing down the street and into the road where a passing car flattened it with a crunch. Michael chuckled and felt his ribs shaking new life into him. He dodged the banana skin which lay in his path and walked under a ladder and grinned, to no one in particular. His car was parked in the lay-by; it had a broken windscreen and a flat tyre. Michael thumbed his nose at it and a loud explosion of a laugh shot out of him somewhere deep inside. A trouser button popped off and his trousers descended with a comical air. Michael shrugged and pulled them up and held them as he walked.

He looked for his victim's van it had disappeared and he wondered how long it had taken, leaving the keys in the ignition would have helped, for once a thief had done him a good turn. He passed the shop and remembered that he needed milk, but the man in front bought the last carton and when Michael went to pay for his paper and cigarettes he realised he must have dropped the wallet when he was knocked over and he burst into paroxysms of laughter, he was so caught off guard that he ended up letting slip to the puzzled shop keeper that it wasn't even his wallet.

He decided he would walk to the park and take a look at the spring flowers. He deftly dodged a roller blader and headed for the walled garden.

When he woke up he was puzzled to find himself in a gown and lying in a hospital bed. A nurse came in and smiled.

'Mr. Murphy sure you're awake at last. Well can I say you are a lucky, lucky man you have beaten all the odds now. The rescuers said that it was a million to one chance that you should have been walking under that tree when it fell on the old walled garden, showering you with bricks. The doctors said with a head injury like yours you'd be lucky to ever wake up again and here you are again proving them all wrong.

Michael smiled to himself. He hadn't a clue what the woman was on about, but if he just kept smiling he'd be fine.

It slowly dawned on him that of course eventually they would find out what he'd done, but it was too late to change a single thing. The man was dead now and that is what he deserved.

All his life Michael Murphy had lived up to his name and had put up with bad luck, the old adage 'what could go wrong would go wrong'-Murphy's Law. It had been a minor irritation really and then something really bad did happen.

He learnt one night what being unlucky really meant. They said she was unlucky that's all, unlucky that she accepted a lift from a man who'd had a few too many and unlucky that the seat belt was faulty, such bad luck. He'd had to identify her body, had seen how her beautiful face had been transformed by hitting the crash barrier. That's how they had explained why her sweet smile was wiped away, but her eyes stared back, intact, challenging him to take revenge.

He'd made her a promise the day she was born, that he would protect her in life. He made another, that he would get his revenge for her death, as he sat in court and watched her killer go free. His previous good record had held the man in good stead; he was fined and inconvenienced by the loss of his license for two years. He'd tried to keep it, said he needed to drive his van containing the tools of his trade as he was a plumber. Her killer walked out of court and back to his life, Michael heard the man's friends saying it was a cause for celebration and promised him a night to remember at their local bar.

Michael's hatred had grown and festered, he'd lost all sense of time without her to make sense of his world. Then one day in the depths of the frosty winter his own bad luck brought him a fair solution. He had woken to the sound of water and found he had a burst pipe. He scoured the phone book for the number and made a sweet request to the man he hated. What plumber wouldn't want to help a poor old man with a burst water pipe?

Waiting for him to arrive was hell. He'd plotted the act down to the last detail. He'd chosen his weapon well. The man could have no suspicions; he wouldn't recognise the address as his daughter had lived with her mother. There were enough Murphys in the town, so no suspicions would be aroused by his name. Michael would make sure this man suffered.

He was punctual Michael had to hand that to him, and he walked in without any problem, didn't recognise the dirty old man, wouldn't have seen any similarity to the smart clean shaven dignified father who'd stared at him in the court over two years ago. Michael had removed her photos which covered most of the walls of his house, in case he saw them. Michael followed him up the stairs and pointed to the cupboard under the sink in the bathroom where he said the stop cock was situated. The man got down on his hands and knees just as Michael knew he would, and as he had planned. Still crouching the man had said 'But there's no stopcock in here' and that is when Michael struck him sharply and firmly on the back of the neck. He was down, but not dead when Michael managed to find the strength to lay him in the bath. Michael tied his hands together and slit his wrists, Michael replaced the bathroom mirror with a photograph of his darling daughter. He wanted her face to be the last thing this man ever saw. The bucket of ice cold water brought him to, for just long enough and Michael was surprised when the man stared at the photograph and shed his last tear.

The nurse showed a young man into the room, 'This is Paul, Mr. Murphy he wants to visit your home to see what adaptations you are going to need You're going to need things like a rail in your bathroom, so you can get in and out of your bath safely. Is it alright if we give Paul your keys, we found them in your coat pocket?'

Michael looked at the man, he was glad it wasn't a young girl; this chap looked as though he could handle things.

Michael smiled and nodded and did a thumbs-up sign. He'd wiped the smile off that plumber and when his mates find out what his fate had been, Michael knew they'd give him a good send off.

Michael heard the nurse say to Paul, 'he's such a sweet old man, to tell you the truth from the state of him when he came in here I don't think having a bath was high in his priorities. Brace yourself Paul for the state of the old fellow's house.'

Michael laughed so much that he cracked a rib. He wondered what would happen to him now. Life was unfair at times, but if he had his way, he'd make sure that people always got what they truly deserved.

Never mind Murphy's Law he thought, as he waited for the fireworks to begin.

FINDAPADDY.COM

'What will I tell June?'

'Is that the best you can say Mammy? I've just told you I've left Paul and all you care about is what you should say to your sister in Cricklewood!'

Anne slammed the door as she stormed out of her mother's house. She had to get away from her mother and her attitudes, which were frozen in aspic circa 1930. She sat on the front wall smoked a cigarette and swore loudly. She knew this would irritate her mother, who always worried about what the neighbours thought. A few minutes later her mother came out, having first checked none of the neighbours were watching.

'I'm sorry Anne; it's just that I don't want to give my old bitch of a sister anything to crow about.'

'I don't want to talk about Aunty 'June', that's not even her real name for Christ's sake.'

'That's typical of her too, wanting a 'sophisticated English name'. Sure, what's wrong with the name Bernadette? And there's no need to blaspheme Anne.'

'I ought to go,' Anne stubbed out her cigarette and threw it on the lawn, her mother retrieved it.

'I'm sorry about your marriage, but I never warmed to him. Thank God your father never lived to see this day.

You know we wanted you to marry a nice Irish boy. Isn't it best to keep the blood pure.'

'Mother, when are you going to realise that the world has changed? You haven't been to Ireland for years you wouldn't recognise it now.'

''Tis an awful shame, didn't we keep our genes to ourselves for hundreds of years.'

'What do you think the Vikings were doing Mammy? Anyway I've told you now, and if anyone wants to know why, you can blame it on bringing me up with the English heathens. Times change Mammy, you and your sister need to move with them.' Anne recognised the faraway look in her mother's eyes. The look she often had when she thought about Ireland and the past.

'Do you remember that nice boy you used to see down at the Irish Association? Declan Doyle, lovely eyes. Good looking boy, he came from a nice family. His uncle was a brain box, wasn't he an Urologist or something to do with brains?'

'A Neurologist Mother, but Declan was no brain box, I can tell you.'

'Then there was Patrick O'Flaherty, he was a good looker now, he had lovely teeth.'

'You make him sound like a horse, Mammy he was gay.'

'Gay? Well he was never miserable and he was always good to his mother. And I remember Martin Shaughnessy didn't he have great curly hair?'

'It sounds like you kept an inventory of them for spare part surgery. If you put their good bits together they would probably make an acceptable man, but the sum would definitely be more than the parts.'

'Come on in now, you'll only have the neighbours guessing there's something wrong, sitting on the front wall swearing and smoking like a hussy!'

Back in the house, Peggy put the kettle on and sighed. The 'phone rang but she let it go to answer-phone, a Christmas present from her son.

'Sure it's only someone trying to sell me something, no one ever calls me.'

Anne knew it was time to leave, once her mother went into martyr and Mother of Sorrows mode.

Once Anne had left, Peggy played the message.

'Hello Mrs O'Driscoll, this is Brendan Doyle calling from Easthorpe Council about *Easthorpe on-line*, please call me on 01376 292929.'

Peggy was perplexed, there seemed to be so many things that bewildered her these days. 'Still, he has an Irish name so I'll call him back.'

Brendan explained that under a new initiative Peggy was entitled to receive a free computer from the council.

'No thank you, sure what would I do with a computer?'

'Come on now Peggy, you sound like a bright young woman to me,' Brendan poured on the charm.

'Huh, I'll be eighty-two next birthday!'

'Go on with you, you sound like a young woman of thirty to me. What part of Ireland are you from Peggy?'

'County Kerry, I came over here in 1938.'

'Listen to me Peggy, you're a Kerry woman and if you had the guts to leave all you knew and come to England in 1938, learning to use a computer will be child's play. Are you in tomorrow?'

The next day Brendan arrived carrying a big box. Peggy thought he was smashing, she noted his lovely delicate ears and rosy cheeks. Once everything had been set up, Brendan had a cup of tea and a piece of Peggy's fruit cake before starting her first lesson.

When Anne checked her e-mails the following week she thought her brother was winding her up or someone was sending her a virus. Before she opened the e-mail from 'Peggy O'Driscoll' she rang her brother.

'Didn't she tell you? Mammy's gone 'on-line', she's only done it to get one over Aunt June.'

Anne opened the e-mail and could hardly believe her eyes her mother was even using icons and signing off as 'POD'. The e-mail explained that a nice young Irish man *'unfortunately he is too young for you and happily married'* was teaching her to use the new computer that the Council had given her. And that she had found a solution to all Anne's problems. 'Come and visit me next week and all will be revealed.'

The following week Anne was unable to park outside her mother's house. When her mother opened the door Anne could hardly believe her eyes. Peggy had had her hair cut and had restored the auburn tint of her youth. She was wearing a black trouser suit, pink top and matching earrings. Anne felt positively dowdy in her jeans and grey fleece. Anne could hear laughter and the buzz of voices, her mother had a full house.

'Here you are then Anne, come in, have a glass of wine. Sure why didn't you make a bit of effort with yourself. You wore those old jeans last time you were here.'

'I would have if I'd known you were having a party.'

'It's a reunion! Come and meet some old faces!'

Anne went through to the sitting room there were five men drinking Guinness, her mother wasn't kidding, they were all in their eighties and nineties. They struggled to get up when she walked in but she asked them to stay seated. Her mother made the introductions.

'Here is my youngest daughter Anne, Anne you must remember Pat Doyle, Declan's father and Michael O'Flaherty, Patrick's father and Gerry Shaughnessy, Martin's father.'

Anne shook their hands although what she really wanted to do was wring her mother's scrawny neck. As soon as she had shaken all the hands and made polite enquiries about their sons she frogmarched her mother to the kitchen.

'So that's your game Mammy, matchmaking! How on earth did you dig that lot up! Some look as though they should have been buried long ago!'

'Sure that's not very nice. I found them at www.findapaddy.com, the website for finding your old Irish Association friends. Hasn't Pat Doyle got lovely ears just like his grandson Brendan?'

'Brendan?'

'Brendan's the one who persuaded me to accept the computer from the Council and he's taught me how to use it. Do you know that there's a web cam in my old home town? I've been watching who goes in and out of Keane's bar all morning. They show you the church on Sundays and there's more in the bar than the church these days.'

'So what about Declan, Patrick and Martin then?'

'I'm sorry Anne, but they're all happily married to nice Irish girls. Never mind, I'm sure with all these web cams and Irish sites I'll soon be able to find you a nice man.'

Anne didn't know whether to laugh or hit her mother.

'Look I'm fine. I'm not ready for another relationship yet.'

'Yes Anne, but you're not getting any younger.'

Anne thought that was rich coming from a silver surfer.

Three months later just as Anne was getting used her mother's e-mails, a letter arrived. She recognised her mother's handwriting and her habit of sticking the stamps on upside down. Her mother's writing looped across the page, telling her about yet another web site she had found about the 'old country' and how she had begun tracing her ancestors on the Ellis Island site. Anne almost missed the final paragraph which was the whole reason for the letter.

'Now be sure to keep the 2nd of June free. Pat Doyle

and I are to be married in Listowel. We will be honey-mooning in the Ring of Kerry. I can't wait to tell June, she won't approve, but then she needs to move with the times. Of course if you can't make it in person, you can always watch our Wedding via the web cam.'

A soft spot for rabbits

Form 4A filed into the biology lab. There was a buzz in the air, 30 pubescent girls were going to get what they had been thinking about for the last six months, they had finally reached the part of the curriculum that was so blandly called *Human Reproduction*. But the girls from the Convent of the Sacred Heart knew this meant just one thing-SEX. Learning more about sex was good enough, but sex as taught by the dark haired, slim hipped Mr. Ashley was just heaven.

Teresa Driscoll looked at her class mates. The starter bras were out in force today pushing whatever development a girl had to the forefront. The skirts had been hitched up an inch or two by rolling the waist band, lip gloss abounded, and eyelashes had been curled. The gymslip army was dressed to kill. A record in the charts seemed to play as Mr. Ashley walked into the room, the Carpenters 'Close to you'. Now they had the desire and all they needed was 'the know how'. Teresa knew they were wasting their time she deserved him and believed he wanted her too.

An image kept playing and re-playing in her thoughts. She saw them sitting under a tree her head resting on his shoulder while he read her poetry. He looked very romantic, even if in real life his true desires seemed to lie in the perfect labelling of the chambers of the heart.

Mr. Ashley coughed and Teresa watched as a fine bead of perspiration appeared on his forehead.

'Good morning Form 4A.'

'Good morning Mr. Ashley,' they replied in sing-song unison.

Thirty pairs of eyes held onto his every word.

'Today we should be covering the topic *Human Reproduction.*' The '*should*' did not go unnoticed thirty pairs of eyes seemed to widen, thirty mouths let out an involuntary *oh.*

He continued, 'Because you are pupils at a Roman Catholic school you are not allowed to learn about human reproduction, the church in its wisdom' did Teresa detect a smirk? 'Has decided, that it is more appropriate to use animal reproduction, as the model for the syllabus. The animal I have chosen is the rabbit.'

Then with a flourish, he pulled down the new rubber blackboard. It revealed a chalk drawing of two copulating rabbits.

There were shrieks of laughter, blushes and giggles. Teresa looked on stony faced she had always liked rabbits, but was not interested in their sex lives. This was it, the moment she made her mind up, she was going to seduce Mr. Ashley and sort the nuns out for once and all.

She listened as Mr. Ashley said that in mammals it was the male that was more dominant in any sexual encounter and that the female was passive and at the mercy of her reproductive cycle. Males were able to tell when to copulate with a female in order to ensure that his genes would be passed on.

Teresa had seen Mr. Ashley snogging Madame Huet the timid little French teacher in an alleyway one lunch time. His hands had been all over her. Teresa knew all about sex, seduction and reproduction. She felt confident enough to teach Mr. Ashley a lesson.

At the end of the class Teresa waited until everyone had left and approached Mr. Ashley, 'Sir I don't think I understood much of that lesson.'

'Teresa, you should have said.'

'And have everyone laugh at me?' She lowered her eyelids and gave Mr. Ashley one of her most seductive looks.

'Would you like to book a tutorial, Teresa?'

'Oh yes please Mr. Ashley' Teresa gushed and gave him her most irresistible smile. She watched where his eyes were focused and was delighted when she realised he was looking at her cleavage. Ah a breast man, she smiled to herself and bent forward to get her diary from her bag providing him with a better view.

She was free at 1 pm the next day, and she smiled her sweetest 'come to bed' smile at him as she left the lab. She had to wash her hair when she got home and think carefully about what perfume she would wear and of course what questions she would need to ask.

The next day Teresa finished her lunch which she had chosen carefully, avoiding any foods that would taint her breath. She had brought her toothbrush and toothpaste with her just in case, and she made her way to the toilet block where she would re do her hair and check her make up and apply more perfume. She rolled her skirt up another inch and undid another button on her blouse. She had worn her most shapely bra, and she had to admit that she looked like every man's fantasy school girl as she made her way to the biology lab.

Mr. Ashley was waiting for her sitting behind his desk wearing an immaculate brilliant white lab coat; it made her think of the dishy Doctor Kildare. He smiled at her as she entered the room.

'Ah Teresa, come on in.'

He pointed to the chair one of two.

Teresa felt nervous now she realised that the lab had windows on 3 sides and she could be seen by anyone who passed by.

'I've a surprise for you in my office Teresa.'

Teresa felt her breath quickening; of course, he had and knew he had an office at the end of the lab which he kept locked.

'I love surprises!' Giggled Teresa.

'Well come along then and as she got up to follow him, the door of the lab opened and Madame Huet came in carrying a cardboard box.

'Ah here is the other half of the surprise!'

Teresa blushed as she noticed a look in Madame Huet's eyes.

She followed Mr. Ashley to his office; Madame Huet sat on the second chair opposite his desk with the box on her knees.

Inside the office was a huge wooden hutch which

housed a very large grey rabbit with floppy ears. Teresa couldn't help but smile, but when she looked closer she realised that the rabbit was not alone, lying next to it were four things that looked like sausages.

'Ooh it has babies!' Teresa unbeknownst to herself, despite her makeup and seductive intentions, at this moment looked like just a sweet innocent 15 year old who loved furry animals.

'Yes hence me choosing the rabbit to explain reproduction.'

'And in Madame Huet's box?'

'The daddy, come and see.'

Madame Huet had taken the rabbit out of the box. She looked at Teresa and Teresa noticed her eyes rested on her hem length and cleavage for a few minutes before she spoke.

'We must keep the male rabbit away from the mother and her babies.'

Mr. Ashley explained, 'Because Teresa, the male would attack and kill the babies and sometimes even just introducing a male may result in the mother killing and eating her own babies.'

'Well humans don't do that, daddies always protect their young, you shouldn't have taught us about rabbits and how they reproduce!'

Mr. Ashley explained, 'The Catholic Church feels that if we teach about human reproduction we are treating the subject too clinically, which is a shame because whilst humans rarely eat their own young, they need to learn that human reproduction celebrates love not sex.

We are superior to rabbits. We make a commitment to our young that transcends the act itself.'

Teresa watched as the pair exchanged a glance which made Teresa feel very uncomfortable. She felt they were capable of looking into her soul.

'Teresa we can explain the act, but not its significance, which is something that some people will never learn.'

Madame Huet smiled at Teresa and said, 'rabbits have sex and humans make love.'

Teresa felt a little affronted now and felt like they were treating her like a silly child, 'Well humans like sex too! There wouldn't be prostitutes and the like if they didn't.'

She stormed out of the room and felt the tears coming as she ran down the corridor and ran straight into Sister Rita, who shouted at her and then she saw her tears.

'Teresa Driscoll, you are wearing mascara.'

Teresa's frustration got the better of her now. 'I have just been made to watch two people having sex, and all you can think of is my mascara.'

Sister Rita went to the biology lab, and did indeed discover Mr. Ashley and Madame Huet in a compromising position in the office. Their expulsion was immediate.

In school Teresa played the victim, but in the early hours of the morning when she struggled to get back to sleep she saw Mr. Ashley's face and heard his words 'love not sex, and we make a commitment to our young that transcends the act itself'.

She doubted that Mr. Ashley and Madame Huet had any knowledge of what she had endured, but she would never let her father force himself on her again.

Breakfast at O'Flaherty's

1998

Brendan O'Flaherty removed the piece of cardboard covering the broken pane in his window and stuck his head out to see what all the commotion was about. A large removal van had blocked the road. Someone was moving into the new bungalow opposite. Brendan disliked all things new. 'What was good enough for my forefathers is good enough for me.' was his motto. According to Brendan new bungalows were the scourge of Ireland. To have new neighbours, in a new bungalow on his own doorstep was abhorrent to him.

The van's sign read 'Reilly's Removals of Renown- Dublin, Liverpool. Birmingham and London- repatriation our speciality.' Brendan grimaced and cursed under his breath. Wasn't that typical! Once the rats had left the sinking ship in droves, and now at the first sniff that things had changed for the better, they were all scurrying back. He watched the furniture being carried off by skittish removal men with tattoos and hair gel. There were leather sofas, marble occasional tables, and a mahogany dining suite, brass beds and boxes by the dozen. The wages for deserting the old country had bought foppish frippery he thought. Finally a computer screen with all its paraphernalia was carried in with great reverence.

'Bah new fangled trickery,' said Brendan and he settled into his favourite chair. He had only a few sticks of furniture yet managed well enough, just as his fore fathers had done. He'd been born and raised in this house along with his five brothers and six sisters. He'd heard the news in town about 'the new bungalow' they said it had five bedrooms, three N-suites whatever they were, a conservatory and study. What would anyone want a conservatory for, unless you were going in for jam making?

The next day there was a knock on his door, he opened it to find a suntanned woman of around sixty pretending to be forty. She was wearing slacks and a jumper with a gold insignia on it, a flamboyant scarf was tied around her scrawny neck and her gold shoes looked most unsuitable for the country roads. She smiled at him.

'Hello I'm Fiona Cholmondey, your new neighbour; I'm the daughter of Kitty Boyle.'

Brendan winced at her accent, took a long look at her and decided he liked her even less than he'd liked her mother.

'Bah,' he said and shut the door. Later he noticed a sign on the Bungalow gate. He fetched his opera glasses and read.

'Backtoouroots- Bed and Breakfast of distinction.'

Outraged, he sat down and wrote to his grandson. Colm was not a bad boy, even though he worked with computers in Dublin. Brendan was flattered that Colm loved visiting his grandfather to 'chill out and get away from it all'. However the last few visits Colm had told Brendan that he was concerned about him, and felt he was getting a little too old to fetch water from the well, and that his failing eye sight would benefit from electric light. Colm kept nagging Brendan to get some work done. However, the water and power companies had made it quite clear; he had refused the 'utilities' for free in the seventies, if he wanted them now he would have to pay.

The next day he found a pink card lying on his mat. He squinted and read, 'Fiona Cholmondey, Sales Ex-eecutive, formerly of Knightsbridge, London. Properties of distinction,' he struggled to read the small print at the bottom of the card, 'New properties considered.'

The talk in town the next day was of Fiona and how her business was aimed at attracting a better class of British tourist for hunting and shooting weekends.' Brendan thought the first thing to be shot should be her.

Colm arrived the next day. That night by the light of the oil lamp sitting in front of the peat fire, he persuaded his grandfather to 'give the woman a chance-there's money in it that could go towards having the water and electricity connected.'

Fiona Cholmondey was feeling sorry for herself. She sat in the kitchen, her new range belting out all the heat it could summon, trying to tune her radio to receive Radio 4. She had been experiencing severe withdrawal symptoms from 'Women's Hour' and 'The Archers' since moving to her Irish idyll. The knock on her door startled her and she was rather alarmed to see the rude old druid from the tip over the road standing on her doorstep. Her reactions were swift; having lived in London she knew better than to open your door to anyone you hadn't known for at least three years. She opened the small window in the study and called to him in her best Irish accent.

'Hello there, is it me you are looking for?'

Brendan heard the disembodied voice and searched for its source. Then he noticed a woman's head poking out from a window at the front of the house. She had a face that would frighten a horse he thought.

'Brendan O'Flaherty, I've come to offer my house for the bed and breakfast.' He answered.

Fiona thought the man was a walking health hazard, but knew better than to alienate the locals

'Grand and how lovely.'

Fiona stared long and hard at Brendan O'Flaherty's thatched cottage, and sighed. She could tell that it would be entirely unsuitable. It was authentic, but who in their right mind wanted to stay in a property that whilst quite pretty, was a crumbling relic? She knocked on the door with her bare knuckles, dislodging the flaking paint as she did so.

The next day a rather formal letter told Brendan 'that unfortunately Mrs. Cholmondey would be unable to represent his home unless extensive modernisation is undertaken."

'She'll have no luck!' Brendan vented his spleen by writing to Colm enclosing the offending letter. A month later Brendan watched a couple in a Range Rover arrive at 'Backtoouroots' with shot guns and thorn proof coats. They seemed to hesitate before ringing the door bell.

The following day everyone in town was full of

it. Prince Charles of England was coming to stay at 'Backtoouroots'. All Brendan could be inclined to say was 'Bah!' Although when he got home he gave his opera glasses a good shine.

A month later Brendan looked out of his window and could not believe his eyes, an army of workmen had descended upon 'Backtoouroots'.

When the work was finished Brendan decided to call on Fiona and take a closer look. The addition of a thatched roof, small wooden windows and white wash, made the bungalow unrecognisable. Fiona was surprised to see Brendan. There was a wonderful smell of baking wafting through the window that evoked fond memories of his late wife. Fiona was surprised to see him.

'Mr O'Flaherty, do come in, sure it's nice of you to call.'

Fiona delighted in showing Brendan her letter from Clarence House. Brendan read about 'Charles' love of traditional Irish architecture', and how he was looking forward to staying in a real Irish cottage.' By the time Brendan had finished reading, he decided that Charles was the first Englishman he could truly like. He returned to his house with half a barm brack and a smile in his heart.

When there was no sight of Charles, and the word in town was of trickery and the folly of Fiona trying to 'make a sow's ear from a silk purse'. Brendan felt a twinge of pity for Fiona whose gifts of brack and potato cakes had brought new warmth into his life.

Brendan opened his door and found Fiona

Cholmondey, resplendent in golfing slacks and cashmere jumper. He blushed and felt inclined to tell her he was busy, only he smelt the unmistakeably aroma of fruit cake and soda bread coming from the plate she was carrying.

'My dear Brendan may I come in and see your delightful cottage once more?'

3 months later

Colm parked his car on Fiona's drive and rang her bell. He glanced over at his grandfather old home with a twinge of nostalgia.

Fiona came to the door and welcomed him in.

'Brendan is just tucking into a plate of stew, come into the kitchen.'

Brendan, like the bungalow had been transformed. He was cleanly shaved and his grey locks had been styled by Fiona's Knightsbridge hairdresser who was a regular visitor. The linen shirt he was wearing brought out the colour of his eyes and the scent of his pomade and aftershave hung pleasantly about him.

'Ah Colm, lovely to see you! As you can see I've got my feet under the table alright!'

'How's the bed and breakfast business going?'

Fiona answered.

'Well Colm, we've Lord Stockbank and a whole shower of them booked in over the summer.'

'And they don't mind fetching water from the well and having no electricity then?' Colm said incredulously.

'Not at all, once the word got out that Charles had been 'up for it', we couldn't keep them away. And I am quite content lodging here. Fiona has to cook for them, but she's paid handsomely for her trouble. Everyone is happy.'

Colm smiled. 'All's well that ends well' he thought. Buckingham Palace had denied all reports that Prince Charles had ever intended to stay at an Irish bed and breakfast. But as usual their denials gave it greater credence. Colm smiled as he thought that in the end new technology had been his grandfather's saviour. Brendan and Fiona had no idea what trickery was possible with a lap top and scanner.

THE CASH COW

Lorraine was driving to work with her radio tuned to the Today programme; she smiled as she heard that the latest research showed that farmers who named their cows had better milk yields. Her long dead uncle would be turning in his grave.

1963

Lorraine watched as her mother peeled off the fivers from the bundle in her handbag and smiled. Her mother could spend it when she had it. Being the only child left at home felt so good at that moment. They went to a Berni Inn armed with their new outfits in bags and ate mixed grills and had Rhum Baba to follow, her mother drank tea, and she was allowed a Coke Cola.

Whilst they ate, her mother ran over their schedule for the umpteenth time. Nora Boyle was so excited and was clearly relishing the thought of their trip home that year.

'Mr. O'Reilly will take us to the station and we'll get a porter to help us with our cases and then once we get to London we will get a taxi to the bus station and take the bus to Heathrow Airport. Imagine us at the airport rubbing shoulders with the stars. We will be met at Shannon Airport by your uncle with the car.'

Looking back Lorraine realises that for her mother who'd only ever known the boat between home and England, the flight from Heathrow to Shannon must have represented a great change in fortunes. Lorraine was eight years old and the youngest of three, and to be honest the mistake of the family. Her mother had recently returned to work and for the first time in their lives money was starting to flow. It was a trickle at first, but the flow was in the right direction at last. Her father could not come with them her mother said it was because his holiday entitlement had been used up earlier in the year, when he attended his mother's funeral. Lorraine now realised that their money would not have stretched to all three of them going away. That is how it was in those days people lived within their means.

A week before they were due to leave the plans changed, they were going to spend the night before their trip in Hammersmith with Aunt Maureen and she would get the chance to see her cousin Bernadette again but really it also provided her mother with an ideal opportunity to show off what her improved financial circumstances were doing for her.

Their holiday was going to be such an adventure, the last time they had been home had been three years ago Lorraine could remember little glimpses of the journey but this year she would remember every detail.

Whilst her mother drank tea with her sister in the Hammersmith flat and boasted, Bernadette and Lorraine whispered in the dark about boys at school and pop groups.

The following morning dawned leaving all a little exhausted, but Mrs. Boyle had unpacked her demure self for the journey. Bernadette's dad found them a taxi and they smiled and waved as the black cab headed for the airport. There was a moment of panic once they arrived with suitcases that needed a porter with none to be seen and with no man to help they struggled, until a nice man offered to help them. Lorraine watched as her mother turned on the charm and beamed at the man. The man was a typical English gentleman who realised that this was their first time at an airport and explained the drill.

Nora Boyle was in ecstasy as she climbed the stairs to the plane. She pointed out the shamrocks on the Aer Lingus plane and delighted in the tiny bars of wrapped soap she found in the lavatory and the little plastic snack tray which she put in her bag to show her mother later. Lorraine thought she was far too deferent to the stewardesses, who seemed to think that they were something special. Then Lorraine was transfixed by the views from the little window and delighted in seeing the cars and houses get smaller and smaller and saw faces and animals in the clouds.

Her mother was strangely still just before they landed, and was muttering the Rosary under her breath. Lorraine was relieved and enjoyed the brief respite from her mother's chatter about all she could see on the plane and her half baked theories about the other passengers.

'He looks shifty that one.'

'Who does she think she is asking for another cup of coffee?'

'Oh wait until I tell my sister Catherine about the stewardesses, proper ladies every one of them. Such an exciting job, dashing all around the world. Of course they are all qualified nurses too you know.'

Lorraine had brought her 'useful bag' with her. A cloth bag made from an old curtain it contained all she would need for the hours she would spend wandering through the fields in search of adventure. It contained her new Agfamatic camera bought for her by her eldest sister (the one with the wealthy boyfriend), string and a hook for fishing, a pen and notebook, a wad of paper and card held together with rubber bands for flower pressing, a handkerchief, pair of scissors and now two small bags of nuts and a plastic cup from the plane.

Uncle Mick was waiting for them when they got off the plane, and Lorraine remembered his small black Morris Minor car with the glued-on statue of the Virgin Mary on the dashboard and the St Christopher medals dangling from the rear view mirror they jingled when he went around bends as she tried to fathom out his impenetrable Cork accent. She was wearing a salmon pink crimplene suit which had been much admired by her cousin Bernadette in London the night before. The journey from Shannon took them through a landscape of wild green scrubby pastures full of black and white cows, rivers spanned by narrow bridges and fields criss-crossed by stone walls.

Lorraine listened in to the conversation in the car,

her mother was sounding more Irish than usual. She listened to Uncle Mick who was married to Catherine her mother's youngest sister, speaking of who had been buried lately. Lorraine hoped they had had been dead first, as they seemed so keen on burying people in Ireland.

The towns they passed through all resembled each other, but seemed to feature brightly painted shop signs in strange curvy writing. Lorraine could smell turf fires which re-stimulated a forgotten memory of her grandmother who wore only black clothes. Memories and questions rose in her mind

They were completely exhausted when they arrived at her grandmother's house. They had to drive up a path with seven gates to open. Her grandmother lived in a small house with four rooms and a small porch which was called the creamery. It housed a very strange metal device which was used to make butter. To a young child from an Essex council estate this second home, her mother's home was like another world, as mysterious and as exotic as any part of darkest Africa or the Souks of Morocco, places which were only glimpsed at in school books. Her grandmother looked strange and when she spoke to her she saw her physically recoil and remark, 'she's more English than Bernadette.' Her uncle PJ lived with her grandmother, he was unused to children she was reminded and was warned to 'leave him be'.

Lorraine had expected to be hugged and made a fuss of, but then no one seemed particularly delighted to see her mother either.

Her grandmother was not like the cuddly ones seen

in story books that dote on their grandchildren; Lorraine tried to get close to her and followed her around the house watching as she went about her daily chores. There was an unchanging pattern to all she did. And there were questions that Lorraine needed to know the answers to, if she was to understand and get to know her grandmother better.

'What are you making Granny?'

'Granny? Sure I'm Grandma.'

'Sorry Grandma what are you making?'

'Soda bread, haven't you seen your mother make it?'

Lorraine shook her head and watched her grandmother knead the bread which she baked on a flat iron in the huge fireplace.

Her grandmother did not appreciate endless questions about her actions.

'Why do you keep a bird's wing by the fire?'

'Why do you put the tea pot on a piece of burning peat?'

'Why are there a brown packages hanging from the beams?'

'Why don't you have electricity?'

'Where do you have a bath?'

'Why don't you wear normal clothes?'

'Why do you have witches caldron's under your drainpipes?'

When Lorraine stopped talking her mother seemed to take over telling stories of household appliances that were transforming her life. 'Imagine having a fridge and a television.'

No one seemed to be that impressed, and no one seemed at all curious about their life in England. Too many miles of differences now separated Nora from her family.

Lorraine overheard conversations, she heard her grandmother tell her mother that she was awful bold and that Bernadette would never dream of asking such things of her. Her mother snapped at grandmother and said it was what came of not getting home enough and that all English children were the same. And Lorraine began to wonder why her mother always told her when they were in England that she was Irish, but now she was in Ireland she had become English. She didn't dwell on it too long because she knew that adults were always contradicting themselves.

Lorraine also overheard her uncle and grandmother talking about her mother, saying how English she had become and she realised that in their eyes nothing could be worse than that.

Bored with the lack of answers and irritated by her uncle's obvious dislike of her mother, Lorraine decided that she would not 'Let him be'. When her uncle returned home that night she watched him sitting by the fire listening to the radio. She could see his dog sitting outside, the dog was not allowed in the house.

'Uncle PJ, why do you call your black dog Brownie?'

He looked at her hard and long.

Her grandmother replied. 'Sure faithen, it's just a

dog; it has no use for a name other than to come when called.'

'And what about your cows PJ what are their names?'

Her uncle shot her a look that would curdle the milk and picked up his stick and went out.

Her grandmother was laughing and Lorraine realised that it was the first time she had seen her laugh and that they thought she was silly.

But Lorraine was not going to be defeated and told her grandmother about her animals at home her guinea pig called Samantha and her tortoise called Toby. Her grandmother seemed most unimpressed.

Looking back Lorraine appreciates now that her grandmother was an Irish Victorian and definitely pre-scribed to the 'children should be seen and not heard' school of thought.

Lorraine decided that she needed to get her uncle on her side and went out to the fields to find him. She saw his cows in the distance and set off to see them instead. They were all black and white but if you looked closely at them you could see they were all slightly different. She set about giving them names, the one with the longest tail she called Bessie and the slow one was Daisy. She had a job thinking of enough names for twenty cows, but she wrote them in her note book with their descriptions to show her uncle later.

That evening after Farming News she opened her note book and read the names to him. He looked at her long and hard then somewhat quizzically, and got up without replying and went to bed.

Lorraine dreamed of pastures and cows running to her when called by their pretty new names, Bessie, Chamomile, Buttercup and Daisy...

The next day her uncle had already left so she went out to find him, she saw him in the distance herding the cows in for milking. He carried a stout stick which he would use to make the stragglers keep up with the others. She followed the muttering man, sneaking up on him with her camera taking his photograph as he went about his work. He was accompanied by his black dog called Brownie.

He ignored her but as she approached him she could see something in his eye which made her mindful of her father when he was in 'one of his moods' and she was wary and stayed some distance from him. Then one cow seemed to resent being herded and turned around and headed back up the field, what happened next has never left her memory. Her uncle seemed to spring to life and headed after the cow screaming at it and calling it names she did not know the meaning of. The cow was stubborn and whilst the other cows continued ambling on to the milking shed this cow broke away at a pace with her uncle in pursuit. He caught up with her with surprising ease and the cow suddenly ground to a halt and turned her head to look at her uncle with a sort of resigned air of defeat. Lorraine watched with horror as he stepped back several paces and took his right leg far back and gave her an almighty kick up the backside, although he probably only kicked her five or six times it seemed to take several hours and she heard herself screaming at him to stop.

'Don't kick Daisy, she just a bit slow.'

He ignored her and carried on until the cow had turned and headed off to the shed. Lorraine ran over to her uncle and screamed at him telling him how cruel he was and how he should treat his own animals with care, and that by kicking a cow he would not get the best out of it.

He did not bother to reply and later when she told her mother what happened she seemed unable to give Lorraine the reply she wanted to hear. The next day her mother got her up early and they caught the bus to town.

The event was never spoken about again whilst they were under that roof.

That night Lorraine listened in to her uncle and grand-mother discussing the cow and talking about the cost of feed and balance of yield. However, the words that really stuck were the ones about herself and her mother, how she was 'a bold, spoilt little English bitch' and how her mother with her 'notions' was herself a sort of cash cow, now that she had been made to return to work.

She thought about Daisy and how she had been abused. She remembered how much they had looked forward to this trip. She thought about her mother sitting on the plane with her fine clothes and she wondered why her mother wanted to come home at all. Although she was unaware of it at the time, she had learned the mean-ing of 'disillusioned.'

And now they were all gone and times were very different. She'd 'turned out alright in the end'; words written on a mass card Lorraine had received from her uncle when her mother died. For a man of few words they spoke volumes.

But she had been right about the naming of cows.

Your Mother knows best?

The young couple were coming to visit Bridie again, not really to see her of course, but to measure-up for curtains and carpets. The girl, Anna, sounded so happy on the 'phone.

'We think it's a sign.' She had said, 'A sort of omen, to move in on Valentine's Day.'

It was a sign of her great age thought Bridie, forgetting it was Valentine's Day.

She let her thoughts wander, it happened a lot lately. She found it strangely comforting that in her thoughts she could revisit places and see again friends that were now no more. She saw a young woman tip toeing down the stairs to be first to get the post, but always disappointed when nothing arrived.

It was probably just as well, her mother would have disapproved of Valentines cards; they would have had to be hidden. Mother had been very strict. She had disliked the modern trend for young couples to meet without being formally introduced. Bridie however had been a rebel and this had made her popular with the boys. Her carefree ways and enthusiasm had always managed to get her lots of partners at the local dance hall and if they did not ask her, she asked them.

Later she joined the civil service and met lots of young

men but unlike her more demure friends, her romances just never seemed to last. Her mother said it served her right, that men preferred the old fashioned girls. Then her brother was killed in the accident and it seemed to set up a series of shock waves, her father died a year later and her mother became ill, there was no more time for dancing and romance. She had done her duty and cared for her mother at home and with the dignity and devotion that her mother expected. The legacy of all this was that now she getting older there was no one to look after her and she was moving into a residential home.

The young couple had great plans for the house. They were going to turn the attic into an office so that Liam could work from home. Anna loved all the 'original features' she was going to change the colour scheme but little else apart from of course the carpets and curtains. Bridie loved to hear their plans for the house. Like her it could do with new life breathed into its old bones. She had become quite fond of the couple; but her mother would have disapproved of them. They weren't married of course and their baby was due in June.

Bridie wasn't bothered, lots of people who were married got divorced these days. She was glad that her mother's morals were no longer held up as the only way to behave. She wished she'd had the freedom that young people had today. Her mother was always lecturing her about morals. Liam was a nice boy, he reminded her of so many of the young men of her youth, with his clean cut features and mischievous sense of humour. The last time they visited he'd kissed her on the cheek and said he wished he were sixty years older because he'd hobble off with her.

At least no one had wanted to 'hobble off' with her mother. Her mother's final years had been very hard. The doctor had told her, that her mother was nasty to her because she was agitated. He felt she had some unresolved issues. She didn't like to tell him, that her mother had always been difficult. Why should she break the habit of a lifetime by evolving into a pleasant old dear?

Valentine's Day dawned and the removal company arrived to take the few pieces of furniture that she was allowed to take with her into the nursing home. Liam and Anna were delighted with the table and chairs, sideboard and other things she had said they could have. Apart from a few small mementoes, papers, clothes and photographs the rest was either being disposed of or had been given to charity.

The taxi arrived to collect her at eleven and her cleaner came at the same time to make sure the place would be spick and span for the young couple. She'd asked Rose to give the attic a good clean as it had not been used for years. She never went up there; it reminded her of her mother too much. Her mother had been a chronic insomniac she used to do her correspondence up there at night. She could still hear the tap, tap of her mothers fingers on her typewriter devising her own particularly acerbic letters of complaint to tardy businesses. As she gave the house a last look over before saying goodbye to it, she realised that there was very little in the house that reminded her of her father.

The residential home was the best she could find; everyone seemed quite lively despite their frailties. There was a bar, which greatly impressed her. The home was owned and run by two Englishmen called Bill and Ben, 'and we're not Flower Pot Men either darling, but we are partial to a little weed.' She had not understood what they meant, but she loved the way their eyes twinkled. Her mother would have been horrified of course, gay was not a word she used often, but she would have written a letter to someone to complain about its new usage. A nice man called Mr O'Leary had been assigned to be her 'befriender' he had a touch of Arthritis he told her and was a widower, he had got fed up of struggling to cook and clean for himself. He asked her if she liked dancing, said there was a Valentine's tea dance that day, except they had no intention of drinking tea. He had winked at her conspiratorially and for a moment she felt she was twenty again. She realised that her home had imprisoned her heart as well as her body for too long. When she got to her room she found her furniture and mementoes waiting for her, Bill and Ben had placed a single red rose in an exquisite crystal vase on her bedside cabinet and had tied big red shiny heart balloons to the end of her brass bed.

The events of the day began to impact on her and she suddenly felt tired, she lay on her bed and dozed. Strangely she dreamed of her father, she saw him returning from work and calling for her. They would walk to the park returning late and incurring her mother's wrath.

She realised that her father had spent very little time in the house he had been out at work, or out with her.

She was surprised to see the young couple when she woke up. They had brought her some flowers, a thank-you for leaving the house in such a wonderful condition. Liam winked as he gave her a big red envelope. A deep blush began to creep from the base of her neck up to her hairline.

She'd been even more surprised when they gave her the bundle of papers; they said Rose had found them hidden in a cupboard in the attic. She recognised the ribbon that the letters were tied up with; she had had those ribbons as a child. When Liam and Anna had left she opened the bundle. A pile of Valentine's cards fell out; she was puzzled, who would have sent her mother Valentine's cards? She was sure her father never had. In fact it struck her that she had never seen a Valentine's card displayed at the house. She opened them looking for names, but in true Valentines' tradition they were not signed, they just contained crosses or question marks. Was she finding out about a side of her mother, she knew nothing about after all these years? Then she found the envelopes the cards had come in. The ink was faded but her name and address was still distinct. Then it dawned on her what Rose had found. Bridie's hands were trembling less from Parkinson's disease, more from anger as she rifled through the pile. There were letters from boys who'd gone to England and America with names she no longer recognised, pouring their hearts out to the happy carefree girl that they'd stolen a kiss from on a Dublin doorstep.

Then she found the carbons of the standard reply letter that mother had sent to them all pretending to be her. The words 'I'm engaged to be married, so regret I am unable to correspond with you further' struck her like a blow to the stomach. How like mother to be so formal and impersonal, tap, tapping the replies in her Victorian tones.

She placed the Valentine's cards on her chest of drawers and thought how at home they looked after all these years. It was too late to get cross with her mother now.

When Mr O'Leary called to escort her to the tea dance, he spotted her cards and flowers and was suitably impressed. 'I can see I've got competition.' He said. Bridie laughed as she took his arm and wondered if she was still up to dancing the tango.

Our favourite haunt

Miss Dunn hated to be the bearer of bad news. The O'Gradys had been caretakers at 'Darjeeling Finishing School for Ladies' for the last hundred years. The O'Gradys had mended beds for royalty, mowed lawns in preparation for visiting maharajas and once had to find additional accommodation on the beach for Sheikh Ali Kazam of Arabia's wives.

It was Sheikh Ali who had been so delighted by the huts, that the first Mrs O'Grady had provided for his harem that he decreed that the exclusive use of a luxury beach hut should be the legacy for all future O'Grady family caretakers. As the hands of the clock approached eleven a.m. Miss Dunn prepared herself for the most difficult meeting of her life.

Marie O'Grady was in good spirits. It was the first day of June and the sun was shining. This was traditionally the time that the O'Gradys opened the beach hut. There would undoubtedly be some work to do, but she loved having her family to stay for the summer.

Miss Dunn took a deep breath when she heard the knock on the door.

'Come in,'

Marie entered dressed in a grey silk blouse and skirt

and last season's darling, a vibrant cerise pashmina. She was unlike any other school caretaker, but then this was Darjeeling School.

'Good morning Miss Dunn, I trust you are well.'

Generations of being surrounded by the world's richest daughters had left its mark on the O'Gradys, Marie spoke with a cut-glass upper bracket English accent; she could blend unobtrusively into any royal court, embassy or country home.

'Ah Miss O'Grady do sit down, tea?'

'Thank you Miss Dunn, but please allow me.'

Marie navigated the silver teapot, cream jug, strainer, sugar tongs and pastry dainties like an ambassador's wife.

But later Marie's spirits were very low as she unlocked the beach hut. It would be the end of a tremendous era; some of her happiest times had been spent in this hut. It was cool and gloomy inside and everything was covered in cobwebs. She donned her royal blue overall and got to work. It was only when everything was 'clean as a whistle' that her family would make an appearance.

'Sure that's better now! It's been a long winter how's my favourite grand daughter?'

Maisie O'Grady, known to all as the Duchess, seemed to materialise out of the steam of the boiling kettle wearing an evening dress and tiara.

'Ah sure now, I've bad news.'

In the safety of the beach hut amongst family Marie

dropped her English tones and sounded more like an Irish washer woman.

'What in this world is wrong with you, you're not, you know? I warned you not to get too close to that dance master.'

'No way darling Duchess and where are the others then?'

Marie was referring to her mother Teresa and Aunt Mary.

'They're still away doing the Winter Season. Getting around to stay with the old pupils is taking longer and longer. One minute it's Gstaad then woof we're off to Mustique or the Sheikh's Winter Palace I can't keep up with it all. Nowhere like home you know. There's no place like my summer haunt.'

'Well dear Duchess, I suppose you thought your days of receiving bad news were over. I'm sorry but I only heard myself today, the school has been sold. By the end of the summer term, I will be without a job and a home and you will be without one of your favourite haunts. Heaven knows who will buy this place and what they will do with it, it could be turned into anything, even an open prison.'

A ghostly wail rose into the air of the hut and zoomed around, causing an unseasonable frost to alight on all the surfaces including Marie.

'And you can stop that.' Marie said with a shiver.

'Don't go giving up the ghost on me; we're going to fight this.'

'But we don't stand a ghost of a chance.' Said the Duchess.

'That's hardly the right spirit. Come on think, we could do with some inspiration.'

'What I need is ice cream, you can't get a good whippy ice in Arabia and I can't think on a see-through stomach.' Said the Duchess as she put on a straw hat and floated out through the walls of the hut. Marie looked at the local newspaper she had bought; Wednesday was 'situations vacant' day.

She suddenly let out a loud ear-piercing scream, the sort you could reasonably expect from someone who has seen a ghost.

'Hey, no wonder Miss Dunn told me this morning she knew it was all over the local paper!'

The Duchess shot back through the wall and peered over Marie's shoulder dripping invisible ice cream down her back. Marie read the headline.

'*Finishing School is Finished Off. Toffs, Told Time's Up For Flower Arranging and Deportment.*'

She read on '*Miss Dunn headmistress admits profits have fallen due to yob culture amongst new upper crust. Reliable sources have informed us that Mystical Molly intends buying the Gothic folly. The T.V. Mystic was seen at Brightrock's most famous School. 'Darjeeling Finishing School for Ladies'. The headmistress refused to confirm or deny this news yesterday. But she did tell our reporter.*

'Fewer gals wish to attend finishing school these days. Rude, spoilt IT girls are all the vogue. They are not interested in how to greet an Ambassador or the correct way to eat Beluga. Our numbers have dropped steadily and we simply cannot carry on. It is all terribly, frightfully sad.' Mystical Molly says she plans to turn Darjeeling's into a horror theme park. She says she has been looking for somewhere like Darjeeling and somewhere really scary to visit is long overdue. 'We have become a nation of wimps. Bring back the ducking stool and the thumb screws.' Mystical Molly has 'foreseen' who will run this amazing theme park so don't bother to apply. But you can see her at the East Pier theatre on Saturday night.'

'So what does somewhere really scary mean? The Duchess asked.'Oh I wish the others were here.'

'She's bluffing just hyping it all up what they call, putting a spin on it.' Marie added in an attempt to reassure.

'Well I have to say, that in all my dead years I've never met a genuine mystic.'

'Well there's always a first time. I think you are finally going to be useful for me. I want that job and if you want to continue visiting this beach hut you are going to help me. But first, let's get the sun cream on and the deck-chairs out. You're looking a bit too ghostly, pale, sweet Duchess. Open the doors and let the summer begin.'

Everything flew into place and the Duchess and Marie settled down to enjoy the sunshine.

'You're right; she won't get me out of this beach hut. Not over my dead body!'

The East Pier Theatre had known better days the great Houdally had performed his famous 'man in a lobster pot escape' in 1920, but it had been downhill since then. Mystical Molly had as part of her plan to curry favour with the Brightrock Town Council agreed to do a free fundraising clairvoyant show for the East Pier restoration fund. As she sat sipping a large vodka and tonic (which she claimed was simply sparkling water) in the dressing room she looked around and regretted her decision. The theatre was distinctly seedy and she found it hard to im-agine that it had ever had a heyday. She picked up the local paper and read the article about her latest venture. This performance in this tacky venue would be worth it, if she could avenge her great grandmother's spirit.

What Mystic Molly did not appear to notice was that the Duchess was sitting on her lap and that her dentures were having a really good soak in the vodka and tonic. The bubbles seemed to be removing the tea stains nicely. The Duchess replaced her teeth and blew Molly a big kiss and returned to the beach hut.

'Well now I know who Mystical Molly is.'

The Duchess appeared so suddenly that she almost caused Marie to upset her jug of Pimms.

'Jesus, Mary and Joseph, oh I wish you wouldn't do

that. You know it takes me time to get used to you after the peace of the winter months.'

'Well what a charlatan, she's the great grand daughter of Dolores O'Dowell and there's nothing mystical about her or her grand daughter! Sure she was helping herself to the School's silver. Funny, you know I've never bumped into her in the spirit world? Perhaps hell does exist. There's nothing we can do till tonight, pass me the Pimms Marie I really need to chill out.'

Marie laughed. She could hardly wait to see what would happen next.

The audience was buzzing with excitement; it was not often that a famous star visited their theatre. There was a hush as the lights dimmed and the Compere announced in a dark velvet voice.

'It gives the East Pier Theatre great pleasure to welcome fresh from communing with the Spirits... Mystical Molly.'

The stage was suddenly lit with hundreds of candles and the audience gasped as Molly appeared dressed in a Victorian bathing suit.

'Good evening Ladies and Gentlemen, and of course we mustn't forget our spirit guests.' Molly stressed 'spirit guests' in her deep velvet voice and paused as if awaiting a response from them, none was received.

The Duchess, who was seated on a rather distinguished gentlemen's lap in a box wearing her best summer frock, rose and took a bow. Marie who had bought an ordinary ticket in the gods smiled but was careful not to wave at her.

'Now let us begin.' Molly surveyed the audience through hooded eyes. 'I see one of our spirits here with us already. He is dressed as a lifeboat man.'

The Duchess looked around her and could not see a spirit matching that description, and thought.

'Huh no such luck!'

Molly undeterred continued.

'Is there anyone here, who had a distant relative who was a lifeboat man?'

Several hundreds of people in the audience shot their hands up. Molly chose a gullible looking woman whom she'd seen earlier in the bar limping.

'It's you dear, this relative was he called, oh it's a little misty, Bill, Phil, Tom, John, Charlie or maybe its Pete or something like that?'

'I did have a second cousin called Bill who was a lifeboat man.'

'That's him; I can see him surrounded by southwesters. He says your limp is getting worse and you should see a doctor.'

And so it went on. The Duchess was fuming. At last she could no longer contain herself, she flew onto the stage and summoning all the energy she could, bellowed into Molly's ear.

'Sure, you're a fraud and a cheat like your great grandmother was.'

But to the Duchess' amazement Molly collapsed and the tatty safety curtain was hastily pulled down.

During the interval Marie and the Duchess plotted their next move. Just as Marie was about to take her seat and the Duchess was seeking a cosy lap to perch on, the scent of camels hit their nostrils and who should waft into the theatre dressed in full Bedouin outfits, none other than Marie's mother Teresa and her aunt Mary.

'Ah sure Marie we've found you!' Marie's mother planted a chilly kiss on her daughter's cheek.

'Your mother was worried about you; we were so surprised not to find you waiting for us at the beach hut as usual.' Aunt Mary blew her niece a camel breath kiss.

'Listen we've got some hard work to do in the second half of this show. We have to save Darjeeling School and make sure that our beach hut remains in our family forever!'

Marie's mother and Aunt Mary looked like they had seen a poltergeist, but with a quick briefing from the Duchess and Marie they were even more than ready for Mystic Molly! Marie took her seat and waited for her to take the stage again.

There were excited whispers amongst the audience as they waited for Mystic Molly to appear.

The lights were dimmed and then a ghostly wail started up quietly and then became frighteningly loud and across the safety curtain a message appeared in shaky writing that appeared like a cloud.

'Who was Dolores O'Dowell?'

The air was heady with a cocktail of spices as Mystic Molly appeared dressed as a belly dancer. She gave her coin belt a 'shimmy' and announced that her spirit guide Fatima, was ready to be asked questions from the audience.

Luckily for Marie, the Duchess, Aunt Mary and Marie's mother a woman in the first row was quick to ask....

'Who was Dolores O'Dowell?'

The audience witnessed Mystic Molly gasp and for the second time that evening collapse on the stage.

The safety curtain fell and 5 minutes later an embarrassed theatre manager emerged to say the show would not continue and a 50% refund would be paid to all.

In Mystic Molly's dressing room the Duchess, Teresa and Aunt Mary got to work on Molly.

'So you can see us then, and do you remember who we are?'

Molly was lying on a chaise longue as white as a sheet.

'Th- th- the O'Grady's.' She had dropped the deep velvet voice and sounded petrified. Her hand shook as she reached for a silver hip flask.

'Yes, and we know all about you and your great grandmother you are both frauds and thieves! Your great grandmother deserved to be sacked and thrown out of Darjeelings.'

'I'm no thief!' Molly's courage was bolstered by nips of Vodka.

'Well I disagree' said prim Aunt Mary, 'you have taken money tonight under false pretences!'

'S'not my fault if people s'are gullible' Molly was beginning to slur her words.

Teresa, cut to the quick. 'Well you've bought Darjeelings with the profit from all of this fakery and we are the real thing. We can do you a big favour and you can help us too.'

Before Molly became too drunk, some smart negotiation took place between the Duchess, Teresa, Mary and Molly.

The future of the beach hut haunt was secure and the following year 'Darjeeling's finishing off School.' boasted real spooks and won the prize as the spookiest place to visit in Britain. But only in summer because: as the Duchess insisted.

'Sure we spirits are awful busy and after all, old habits die hard and sure we have our standards and still have to do the Seasons.'

Marie kept Molly in line, and even managed to retrieve some of Darjeelings' long lost silver. The finishing off school was not quite the place that Darjeelings had been, but as long as she had her beach hut and her family around her she was happy.

Spanish Point

'I'm sorry Marion but your father and I think it's for the best.'

Her mother's words had stung her deeply; she had been told that their summer holiday was cancelled, but not the reason. It was too awful for a seven year-old to cope with.

'But why?' Marion had sobbed. She lay on her bed and had cried softly, as she listened to her parents' whispers. She would be the only girl in the class not having a holiday that year. It was bad enough that she was so different from all of her friends. They lived in smart new houses and had brothers and sisters all she had was this small bedroom in the terraced house where her dead grandmother used to live. She asked so many questions but never got the answers. She did have her special friend Miss Carrie, but her parents frowned upon this and cruelly called her 'Marion's imaginary friend.'

Marion could however rely on her friend who at this very moment was singing her a lullaby and soon she was fast asleep.

But things got worse; her mother was rushed into hospital without any explanation. When her father told her he was taking her to Aunt Bridget's house in Clare, she knew that throwing another temper tantrum would not work. His face had that really serious look that grown-ups have when something bad is happening. She had seen that face many times.

They set off on a soft day leaving Dublin and all she knew. She thought of her friends flying off to Spain to their second homes and wondered why she had been so unlucky to get the parents she had. She felt guilty for thinking these thoughts and would have to confess all to the priest at her next confession.

Aunt Bridget was her mother's eldest sister and lived by the sea and painted pictures. In her paintings it was always hot and sunny and they always seemed to include the most perfect looking family having fun on the beach, a tall handsome man, a slim blonde woman, a boy who looked about 10 and a girl about her age having fun on the beach. They had a lot of Aunt Bridget's pictures at home and Marion used to stare at them and wish that her family was more like the people in the paintings.

The weather improved and by the time they got to Limerick it was sunny and warm. Neither Marion nor her father fully appreciated it; they were quiet and alone with their thoughts. There were things that Marion longed to know, but was too young to know how to ask, and too young to hear the answers. Her father looked pale, and she thought his eyes looked strange and shiny. When they got to Spanish point the surf was up and the sun was sparkling on the water, the beach looked inviting with plenty of children to meet and play with. But when her father said he could not come in with her, as he needed to get back to Dublin as soon as possible Marion suddenly felt abandoned and so alone. Aunt Bridget made a big fuss of her but she watched as her aunt hugged her brother-in-law with a serious face and said something about luck and God's lap. There were anxious looks back at her and more whispers and then her father came back and hugged her again.

'Now be careful and do whatever Aunt Bridget says and don't go near the sea on your own.'

His parting words bounced off her like all of his other warnings, adults were such kill-joys. His tears were wet on her cheeks.

The seagulls called to Marion and to her their eerie cry told of the cruelty of the sea, she watched her father's car disappear along the headland. Once her father's car was out of sight her aunt wore a face that tried to look jolly. 'Don't worry Marion everything will be grand I'm sure. Now this way you get a holiday by the sea too.'

Marion smiled at her aunt out of politeness, but what fun would it be all alone in this cottage with her aunt for the summer. Aunt Bridget had grey hair and looked old. She had a husband and children once, but lost them, her Mammy had said. Marion knew this made Aunt Bridget sad. Marion could remember getting lost in the supermarket and her mammy had howled and howled when she was found. She knew that losing people made you sad.

Aunt Bridget lived in a damp cottage with 'night storage heaters' which made no sense to Marion. The room she was shown to was pink and looked like another little girl had just popped out and would return at any moment. There were clothes in the drawers and the wardrobe, old fashioned clothes and Marion struggled to find space for the things her father had hastily thrown into a suitcase for her. Miss Carrie was most unimpressed and refused to unpack her rucksack.

While Aunt Bridget cooked supper Marion explored the rest of the cottage. There were three bedrooms upstairs; the largest was Aunt Bridget's which she did not enter, the third room was full of boys' toys mostly boats and airplanes which hung from the ceiling. The bed was made and the room smelled of glue, she hurried out feeling uncomfortable amongst boys' things.

They ate supper in silence, her aunt seemed unable to think of anything to say and Marion was happy to escape to her room to read the 'Swallows and Amazons' books that seemed to fill the book shelves. Miss Carrie was sulking and refusing to do anything, except insist that they should return to Dublin. Marion told her to 'go to sleep, tomorrow is another day.'

The next day was cold, they went to a deserted little beach near the cottage and she was left to make sandcastles, as long as she promised not to go near the water. She would play with Miss Carrie. Miss Carrie was green and no one else could see her. Her mother would not let her play in the street at home so Miss Carrie had become her best friend. Marion did not see the other girl until she lost her bucket.

Marion had been making a large castle with a moat

and was going to the edge of the sea to fetch water. A sudden gust of wind blew her bucket along the beach so she gave chase. It was blown into the sea, so she went into the water to get it. The water was cold and icy. She felt a shiver run up her spine. Then suddenly there was someone behind her, who touched Marion on her shoulder.

'Stop Marion.'

Marion screamed and turned to see a blonde girl about her age standing behind her.

'The sea is a dangerous thing.' She stared at Marion with familiar pale green eyes.

'My bucket I must get it.'

'It will suck the air from you.' The girl then turned and looked at the bucket. The bucket stopped floating out to sea and seemed to glide back to Marion. She bent down to pick it up, and then turned to talk to the girl, but she had gone. She went back to her sandcastle, sad that the girl had disappeared; it would have been nice to have another friend. Miss Carrie told her not to worry she was still there.

Then her aunt called her in to lunch.

Whilst eating ham sandwiches made with delicious white bread not the heavy brown bread she had to have at home, Marion thought about the girl. She hoped she would come out to play after lunch and thought about games they could play. Aunt Bridget looked sad; she had spent the morning in her studio. Suddenly Marion found herself asking if she could see her aunt's latest painting.

She did not know why she had asked; she just found the words slipping out of her mouth. Her aunt's reply had shocked her.

'No, I cannot show anyone. It's too awful; no one's eyes should have to see what I have seen.' Her aunt burst into tears and ran from the room. Marion felt desperately sad and alone. Her tears ran in rivulets down her cheeks landing on her half eaten sandwich making it soggy. There was a tap on the window; the girl was there. Marion dried her eyes on her napkin and smiled. The girl beckoned to Marion and she got down from the table and slipped out the backdoor. She did not want to disturb her aunt so left without saying anything.

The girl led and Marion followed, on and on they walked away from the house away from the beach away from anything familiar to Marion. When she stopped and looked back, knowing she should not be going, the girl would call her and Marion followed. The sun had come out and it was hot and the road ahead was shimmering, and she did not see or hear the car as it came towards her and neither did the girl. Suddenly a man was pushing her away from the road and onto the grass. He was tall and blonde. She landed hard bumping her head on a rock the next thing she heard was the man telling the girl off.

'Lou-Anne be more careful she could have been killed.'

The girl turned and looked at Marion, she watched Marion's blood seep from a cut in her forehead.

'Come Marion.'

Marion wiped her head with her sleeve and got up and followed the girl.

Back at the cottage, Bridget had gone to apologise to Marion but found no sign of her in the house. She had abandoned her lunch and was no where in sight. Bridget ran up and down the beach shouting for Marion. What was happening? Her sister's news had upset her, what if she lost her sister's child too? She found the abandoned bucket by the water's edge and broke down. It was happening again. It was all her fault. The tape in her mind rewound and played again, rewound and played again.

The little boat looked inviting. It was wooden with a single mast a perfect boat for a child. Marion traced its name 'Otter' with her finger she liked the name.

'When can we have a sail in it?' The girl was not listening. Marion suddenly realised that she did not know where she was and that her aunt would be cross.

'I need to go; my aunt will be worried she will miss me…'

A man appeared. It was the man who had saved her. Marion smiled at him and said 'Hello' but he ignored her. The girl suddenly seemed to become animated and Marion's head hurt and she stumbled backwards, it felt like she was watching a film.

'Can we go Dad please, just a quick sail around the bay Otter' looks perfect. Pleeeease.'

'There's a storm brewing it's not safe Lou-Anne.'

'Here's mummy look.'

Marion looked in the direction that the girl pointed. She gasped; it was Aunt Bridget or at least someone who looked a lot like her. This woman was younger, she was blonde not grey, she was smiling and looked beautiful. She had the same pale green eyes as the Lou-Anne.

'Hi there.' The woman said. 'Look at *Otter* it's beautiful, Bill certainly has made a good job of restoring it.'

'Can we take it out Mammy? I'm dying to have a sail in it.'

'I said no Lou-Anne. I can feel a storm brewing.'

'But it's a lovely day Mike.'

'You don't know this bay like I do. A storm can just come up out of nowhere. You know the history of Spanish point and the wrecked ships from the Armada.'

'But that was centuries ago with old boats, you can get back; you don't have to go far.'

Marion began to cry but no one heard or even noticed her.

'Oh alright, just a quick once around the headland.'

Marion fainted.

Bridget cradled Marion both terrified and relieved to find her.

'Aunt Bridget where am I? The boat?'

'I found you lying here on the roadside. Doctor Riley's on his way, he said not to move you.'

Marion drifted off again, and saw the woman wave Lou-Anne and her husband off, as they sailed towards the headland.

When she woke again Marion realised she was back at her aunt's cottage and was lying on the chaise longue in her aunt's studio, her aunt's canvases surrounded her. The smiling happy faces were now very familiar to her.

'Any news of Mammy?'

'Yes darling, your mammy is fine and you have a new baby sister. The doctor says that all you have is a couple of grazed knees and a bump on the head.'

'A baby, was that what it was all about?'

'Yes darling, she's very little but doing well. Your daddy is coming to collect you tomorrow.'

Later when her aunt had crept out thinking she was asleep, Marion got up and walked over to her aunt's easel. It was draped in a cloth, slowly and carefully she lifted the edge of the cloth to look at the painting underneath. This painting was unlike any of aunt Bridget's other paintings, it was dark and gloomy there was no blue sky, yellow sand and blue sparkling water. At first she couldn't see any people in the picture. It was a picture of a tremendous storm. A boat was being tossed in the gigantic black waves. Marion peered closely at the boat's name-plate *Otter* it said. She could see three figures crouching in the boat. Her eyes searched the canvas further and saw that there was a fourth person. A woman stood on the shore, her mouth was open, Marion had heard that scream.

They had to wait weeks before the baby was allowed home. When Marion was allowed to hold 'Baba' as they called her she opened her eyes and revealed surprisingly for a newborn, the palest of green eyes. The words popped into her mouth and were spoken before she could stop herself.

'Let's call her Lou-Anne.'

Her mother looked shocked and quickly looked at her sister.

Bridget smiled and looked happy.

'Yes that's a wonderful name.'

Some months later as she played with her little sister, Marion realised she hadn't seen or thought about Miss Carrie for months.

ONCE UPON A TIME THERE WAS A TOILET FAIRY

A toilet fairy's life may not seem glamorous, but to me it is almost perfect, because I live with James at 'Moonlight Cottage'. I cook, clean and shop for him but he doesn't know I exist.

My name is Tina toilet fairy by the way. And James has certainly changed since I came into his life. I found James at the top of a garden; I had run away from home after a lover's quarrel with a sprite with the unromantic name of Ron. I could tell James had a good heart, even if he did have what some would describe as a 'pizza face' and a love of anorak coats, but I know the 'silk purse from sow's ears' spell so I transformed him. He also lived in a very untidy flat which; 'boasted' mushrooms around the bath and lime scale encrusted toilets.

Anyway, back to me. I'm the one that cleans the toilets and ensures that their lids are always put down, that's where I get my name. I also clear away breakfast things and make beds. At first, James did notice something was different, but now he takes his good looks, tidy home and sparkling toilets for granted. He just comes in and pats the laughing Buddha in the hall. He thinks it is the stuff from the Feng Shui catalogue that changed his luck. And after all his favourite childhood story was 'The ugly duckling'. It is amazing what humans believe in!

But it's all my work and what for? I love him, but he loves someone else. It's not fair being a fairy, people only ever think of us at Christmas time. We are alright to put on the top of trees, but then we are put away again without second thought.

I wish I hadn't overheard that telephone conversation. The words keep going around my head, like bees in a foxglove. Gosh this mirror is filthy. Look at me, hey Feng shui mirror, what do you make of me?

'You're not bad looking, but you could do with a makeover. Have you ever seen 'Groundforce'?

'I'm a toilet fairy, not a water feature and I need more useful advice. Be quiet or you will be smeared for life.'

'Sorry, I thought looks mattered, otherwise there would be no need for me.'

'I like my blue hair and matching gossamer dress, even if it is impractical for housework, it makes me feel more feminine. I'm only a toilet fairy; I don't move in royal circles and hang out at christenings. Anyway he can't see me, and it's too late anyway. Do you listen into 'phone conversations too?'

'No, I just watch the hall and try and keep the riffraff out. But I have seen his new girlfriend. Much better skin than the others.'

'You've seen her? I must find her and talk her out of this, tell her the truth.'

'So what did you overhear?'

'James has asked his girlfriend to move in and he hopes she will marry him.'

'But if she does James will return to the state he was in before I found him.'

'You mean he will start squeezing his spots all over me again? This is serious!'

'I love James whatever he looks like, but once a human marries him my magic will not work. What can I do?'

'Don't ask me, life is much simpler when all you do is reflect others views.'

'I wish James could see me, then I could tell him I love him. I wish I could tell him that I have been looking after him for years. He doesn't need a wife, he has me.'

'Only two wishes? Why waste time on men, they are really vain. I should know.'

'I wish James was a fairy, but he isn't'

'Look there was something I did hear. She is a solicitor and she works for a company that's got a name like 'Right', James made a joke said she was the right woman for him. It made her giggle.'

'It should be me giggling with James; the address will be in the book with the pretty yellow pages.'

'Well yellow means happiness in China, good luck.'

I do feel a bit silly hovering outside 'Wright and Partners Solicitors'.

That must be her. I'm going in!

'Clare are you going to do any work today?'

'Sorry Sue, but I feel like I'm in a dream. James has asked me to move in.'

'Are you sure that's not a nightmare? When you work with divorce all day it's hard not to be cynical. But I

have to say, he has been good for your skin- you're looking great'

'It's like a fairy tale.'

'Oh dear you do have it bad. Well I hope there is a
happy ending, and that he doesn't believe in toilet fairies,
self-loading and unloading dishwashers, not to mention
homing pigeon underpants that fly into laundry baskets.'

'Well I do, why shouldn't he?'

Ah If only they knew, but how does this Sue know
about what I do? Clare is pretty, but look at those long
nails! I can tell she doesn't like housework. Poor James.

'Anyway Sue, James is a wish come true. I have a tur-
key wishbone to thank. My mother said it was so large
that I could safely make three wishes. And they have all
come true.'

Feng shui and now wishbones, sometimes I think humans are very silly.

I'm going back to Moonlight Cottage; it's going to be
harder than I thought she's under someone's spell.

'Hi mirror I'm back.'

'At last, there's a very strange fairy in the kitchen looking for a pumpkin.'

'Ooh there's only one person that could be, Libby my
Godmother.'

'Now Tina I have been watching you, and I can't say
that I like what I've seen. When are you going to spread

your wings and stop believing in those out-dated fairy stories? I bought you a book a while ago, did you read it?'

'Oh you mean that one about Cinderella's complexion?'

'You haven't read it have you?'

'Sorry I've been too busy looking after James.'

'Now my dear, you should have known that James would meet a girl and fall in love.'

'But I love James. He is all I wished for.'

'You should have left him the way he was. And sent him out in dirty shirts, that he has to pick off the floor where he has left them. Surely no girl in her right mind would fancy him, once she had seen his smelly flat and filthy sheets.'

'Sorry Libby, but have you ever been in love? I did those things because I loved him and what other work is there for fairies these days? All those pesticides have driven us into the service industry.'

'Ah but look at me I was happy making my own wishes come true until the credit crunch ruined everything. The money market was easy for us fairies, we have always been good at predicting futures, but now I'm back to helping hapless girls find their princes again.'

'Well serves you right Libby and Clare has a good reason to believe in fairy tales.'

'Well, Clare is in for a shock. Imagine marriage without a wand! It will be no fairy story, when all they discuss is spot cream and whose turn it is to put the bins out. Now find yourself a new job.'

'Yes Libby.'

'You know you lost Ron, because of your lack of ambition. What Sprite wants his wife cleaning toilets for idle humans?'

'Ron should have loved me the way I was and stopped trying to change me. Besides, I need someone more down to earth.

'But James doesn't even believe in fairies. We all need someone to believe in us, or we must believe in ourselves. You could go to the top of the tree if you wanted to. These days we've got to write our own stories, or someone else will. Got to go, I've just predicted a run on the dollar.'

'Bye Libby, but don't forget *money can't buy you love*'

'Ok, mirror, how do I find another job?'

'I've always wanted a job in a ladies sauna, but the steam would be bad for me. But you know he is not married yet, I'd go shopping, buy myself some new clothes; that wildwood Titania look is so dated dear. Have you tried Ghost?'

'Do you think so?'

'I know so; it's all minimalist now, or 'floaty' see-through numbers. Then take a holiday, chill out on pollen wine, rest your wand and I bet while you are away, this girlfriend will see the real James.'

'Oh mirror there's more to you than meets the eye!'

'My pleasure, buy some books too. I've heard

'*Why men can barbecue and witches just fry.*' is a good beach read. And '*The hunk at the top of my garden – a guide to enchanting men.*' could come in very useful.'

<u>Six months later.</u>

Well I am back at Moonlight cottage and it looks remarkably tidy.

'Well met at 'Moonlight Cottage' at last fair Tina, had a good holiday?'

'Ron what are you....?'

'Oh you could say I'm 'moonlighting', from the Christmas ornament business. I've been Claire's handy sprite for a while actually. They are getting on really well; I've permanently cured their spots by the way. You look great too!'

'Well Ron, you've changed too.'

'Handy work tones you up. Your plan has failed Tina'

'So, what happens now?'

'If this was a story, I would take you in my arms and kiss you. We would get married and live happily ever after. Make a wish; have me for life not just for Christmas.'

'But fairies can't make their own wishes come true, it's against the rules.'

'Tina, let's make each other's wishes come true.'

'Aren't you worried that my wishes may be different to yours?'

'Reading your mind Tina, I can tell we are going to live happily ever after.'

Ron was wrong because little did he know that at that very moment the man of my dreams was away fetching his crock of gold. I suppose you'd call me a gold digger but with my new leprechaun beau, I didn't have to do any of the digging!

Ron should never have told me my work was demeaning, any sprite who only works once a year puts a dress on, and sits on the top of a spiky tree should keep quiet about career choices!

No more jobs at Woolworths

Wait till she gets in the little madam! I'll give er what for. I've just had the school on the 'phone that snooty secretary rang me to say

'Ms. Finch your daughter Kyley has not reported for registration and is marked as absent can you confirm this please.'

All hoighty, toighty like. And I rings Kyley's mobile and she don' answer it. It was er mock maths GSCE today, and she bunks off! I've been telling er that in my day if you don't get your CSE's at least there was always jobs at Woollies. Well not anymore! I know what she'll say about er phone, outacredit!

Well here she is!

'Right madam, you can get upstairs and clean your bedroom, cos you are well out of order.'
'But Mum.'
'Don't you, but mum me, upstairs young lady and get cleaning.'

Well that told her! I need a fag!

I look at job ads in the local paper. At least I'm ok, plenty of work for care assistants, loads of bums need wiping! I wanted something better for Kyley. She's a bright girl, but it's the same old same old, like me she's discovered boys! And now it's make-up and dates are all what matters. She keeps asking why we aven't got a computer, says she's deprived cos she can't go on msn and facebook like Jade. Well Jade's mum and dad are loaded and I struggle wiv no support from Kyley's dad. It's down to me her success or failure. Me mum and dad try to help, but they were never the brightest tools in the box and look what I turned out like!

An yes I ended up working at Woollies and my friend Shirley worked at the Bata shoe factory. Those with a few CSEs did secretarial courses and went up to London on the train to work for Commercial Union but it was rich usbands we all dreamed of, a rich guy who would buy you a house, take you on holidays to Spain and ban you from working ever again. Ah but it never appened to me, pregnant at 17 with Kyley's big brother and look what became of im! I hears nuffink from im and that's the best way for things to stay. Bad news just like his bloody father.

And who is this at the door? Oh my God it's the Old Bill, what the ell has she done now?

'Ms. Finch?'

'Yes'

'Mother of Kyley Finch?'

'Yes and what the ell has she done now?'

And they tell me somethink so amazing! I am gob-smacked and then I feels so guilty like. So I call up the stairs in my sweetest voice.

'Kyley love, come down here please.'

Here she comes and God do I feel bad.

'Kyley, love why didn't you tell me? The Ole Bill was 'ere.'
'I tried to but you were that mad that you couldn't listen, my room is tidy anyway.'
'Come ere.'
I cuddle 'er and she bawls.
'Here sit down wiv me and tell me all about it.'

'I was on my way to school right, and you know Acorn way, well there's this man right, in his pyjamas staggering around, he was well old.'
'Was anyone else about?'
'No that was what was well weird like, the place was deserted, jus me an this ole geezer.'
'What did you do?'
'Well when e sees me e gets all excited like, pointing to me and trying to say stuff but when e tries to talk I don' understand a blooming word he says, es got some sort of odd accent, then I realise es Irish.'
'Irish in Acorn way?'

'Yeah he looked about 90.'

'Oh my God that's Mr. O'Conner, e's had a stroke'

'Yeah that what the amblance man told me.'

'So what appened next?'

'Well I tried to calm im down got im to sit on his garden wall, but he was finding it ard to breathe, e kept trying to tell me somethink.'

'What like?'

'E said or it sounded like his wife was out and it was cold. He looked real bad so I phoned 999 from my mobile.'

'Oh Kyley I'm so sorry I ad a go at you.'

'Well the amblance was on its way, but I couldn't just leave im there, could I? I knew I'd miss my exam but I thought whatever! It's only a mock.'

'What appened next?'

'Well he kep trying to tell me to go into his ouse but I wasn't aving none of that.'

'Too right! An then?'

'The amblance came and they checked im over and tole me he'd ad lots of strokes and tole me he would be ok now. They was taking him to Basildon ospital. But he was aving none of it, he kept pointing to his ouse and I told the amblance people that e'd kep trying to tell me somethink about his wife being out in the cold.'

'Oh Kyley my love.'

'What is it?

'The ole bill tole me what you did, and tole me what appened next.'

'What appened?'

'You went off and when the amblance men went into is ouse they found is wife dead on the floor, she'd ad heart attack.'

'Oh my God.'

'Yeah but you did a good job my love.'

'Yeah but that poor old man, what's gonner appen to im now?'

'Ole bill said his daughters are looking after him now, I knew is daughters right snotty cows they were too. The local Comp wasn't good enough for them, they went to that private Convent. They don't live around ere no more.'

'Well Mum who can blame em eh?

'It's not that bad Kyley, is it?'

'Well mum I've bin finking, I felt really sorry for im and I did the right fing by im.'

'Yeah Kyley I'm proud of you.'

'So you see I've made my mind up, I'm going to work real hard now and become a nurse.'

'A nurse?'

'Yeah why not eh?'

And I thinks to myself it's an ill wind...

'Cos mum there ain't no more jobs at Woollies!'

Yeah says I to myself, but you were too good for Woollies anyway!

But later I finks to myself what was she doing all afternoon?

The Wine, the Witch and her Wardrobe

Mary sat alone on the sofa in the conservatory sipping a glass of wine, it was Halloween and this was the first year that she hadn't even bothered to carve a pumpkin. She could see the flames from next door's bonfires and imagined the children dressed up and having fun. Her children were leading lives of their own now and her husband Niall was gone. Not passed away, no far worse he was happily married to her 'best' friend Eilish and was living in the splendour of a mansion in Blackrock. Eilish had done very well out of her divorce settlement, Mary wished she could say the same. Niall always called Mary an old witch, but if she had been a witch she would have turned Niall and Eilish into toads long ago.

She walked to the hall and looked at herself in the mirror; she wasn't that bad looking for 48. She had a few bulges around her middle, but her legs were shapely and her breasts weren't that saggy. She could probably find another man if she tried hard enough, but she was fed up of men, she had been betrayed by her husband and hurt so badly. She had told her friends that in future all she needed was a man who could be kept in her wardrobe, to be taken out whenever she needed him. The man would be returned to the wardrobe when he stopped being useful, where he would have to wait until she needed him again.

She continued gazing at herself in the mirror and then remembered an old wives tale about making a wish on All Hallows eve. She felt daft but there was no one to overhear or see her.

The next morning the alarm went off at the usual time. Mary dragged herself to a sitting position and then she caught sight of herself in her wardrobe mirrors and couldn't believe her eyes. Her hair was long, black and glossy and when she lifted her long white cotton night-dress she found that her slightly past its best body had been replaced by a body that Elle Macpherson would be envious of. Then she noticed that her bedroom was stacked with boxes and when she opened one she saw that it was a case of 12 bottles of the finest Chablis. There was a note in the box-

'Mary be careful of what you wish for...

Now drink and be merry ...

Stop   drinking   and   you   will   age...
DRAMATICALLY!

Now lie back and let Rupert do his magic'

Mary was very puzzled she was actually being told to drink and who was Rupert?

As she said the name Rupert out loud, her wardrobe door burst open and a tall, athletic, handsome blonde man stepped out carrying a bottle of Champagne and a dozen pink roses, he was naked and very pleased to see her!

After making love Mary opened her wardrobe and without being asked Rupert climbed back inside. Mary went back to bed to recover then realised that she was running late for work. She phoned the office and tried to speak but found that she no longer sounded like the old Mary, she now had a silky honeyed voice that promised seduction and pleasure to all. Jane on the switchboard took the message and said,

'I'll pass the message on but I only wish I had the throat infection that you've got!'

Mary realised that she hadn't needed to speak to Rupert because their love making had been so instinctive. Rupert knew what turned her on and needed no instructions. Perhaps any conversation with a man who lived in her wardrobe would be a little pointless and probably very dull. She had not fully realised the perils of 'not getting out enough'.

She caught sight of herself in the mirror and was horrified to see fine lines beginning to creep across her face. She went downstairs to the kitchen which over night had warped into something from 'Homes and Gardens.' She was delighted to see that one entire wall was now devoted to a large wine fridge with glass doors; it was full of fine wines of excellent vintages. Someone knew her taste in wine very well, she opened a bottle of white Bordeaux and went in search of some Crème de Cassis. When she opened her kitchen cupboards she discovered that all of the boring boxes of cereal and pasta had been replaced with every possible type of mixer and an array of wine based spirits. She mixed herself a generous Kir and took a large swig in front of her hall mirror which had been transformed into a Rococo wonder.

Then she realised that she no longer lived in a little semi detached estate house in Dublin 7 she looked out the window and realised that she was living in a castle in Killiney. She wondered how she would be able to pay the electricity bill as she counted the ornate chandeliers that hung from every ceiling. She raced around the castle switching them off. When she went to look for her wallet she found that her Dunnes store bag had been replaced by the latest Jimmy Choo and inside were a handful of letters and a Chloe wallet stuffed full of 100 euro notes. The letters were statements from her bank she almost fainted when she read the balance of her account, then she made a point of switching on every light and she turned the heating up to the maximum temperature too. She composed her resignation letter in triumph, but rushed to have another drink when she noticed that a crop of age spots had appeared on the back of her hands.

A little worse for drink she climbed the stairs to her bedroom which had been transformed too, now she had a large dressing room which contained several walk in wardrobes. She wondered which one contained Rupert so she called his name and nothing happened; a little surprised she wondered what would happen if she called out another man's name. She had always been rather attracted to a guy called Otis at the office. So she called out this name and one of the wardrobes slid open to reveal the exquisite young man, he held a plate of smoked salmon and caviar blinis in one hand and a bottle of Pink

Champagne in the other. He smiled and blew her a kiss and just like Rupert he was naked and had everything in the right place and plenty of it too!

Their love making was so vigorous that a rather lovely Vermeer that hung behind her beautiful Bateaux Lit bed fell off the wall somewhat concussing Otis.

'What I need now is a handyman.' and no sooner than the words had been uttered than another wardrobe slid open to reveal a rather muscle bound man wearing nothing but a tool belt. He made short work of replacing the hook to hold the painting and then noticing that Otis had recovered she allowed both men to satisfy her whilst she sipped some Champagne having noticed that her left breast was beginning to sag.

Thirty minutes later she opened her wardrobe and both men dutifully climbed back in.

Mary checked her new Cartier watch it was only 11 am but she was absolutely exhausted.

'So' pondered Mary, 'I can have every kind of man I have ever wanted hovering in my wardrobe, I have enough wine to last a lifetime, I am beautiful, rich but actually I need to get out more. What is the point of being so rich and beautiful if just me and a handful of my fantasy men know about it?'

The strange thing was that despite looking beautiful and having huge wardrobes Mary was still wearing the long white shapeless winceyette night dress. She decided it was time to hit town, so she called out,

'Jeeves run my bath please'.

Then on cue a man in full Butler attire emerged and

did just that, before offering to pour her a large glass of chilled Chablis.

In her marble claw foot bath Mary thought about what the evening ahead would hold, she hoped that a rather flash sports car must be garaged somewhere in her extensive grounds. She imagined herself driving to the city, it would be too cold to have the top down, but she would be wearing something fabulous. The dilemma she faced was, should she go alone or bring one of her fantasy men with her? She decided that there was no point going out to flaunt her new gorgeous body, fantastic car and obscene wealth if she could stay at home and make love to the same man.

She called for a make-up artist and hair dresser. Two cute gay guys arrived with pink fluffy towels and did her hair and make-up.

When she was looking fabulous, she opened her wardrobes to see what gorgeous outfits awaited her. To her amazement there were no clothes but lined up appearing to sleep standing up like horses, were men of every kind imaginable. There were naked plumbers, electricians, gardeners and even one man wearing a lanyard around his neck that stated he was a Vice Consul! However not one single outfit was in her wardrobes she questioned the gay guys but they just shrugged and climbed in next to the Consul guy!

'Vice is nice' they whispered to the frightened looking man.

And 'Be careful what you wish for Mary...'

Undeterred Mary finished her Chablis and marched

out of the castle and it didn't take her long before she found the stables that luckily for her did not contain horses but instead had 5 sports cars lined up and all with their keys in the ignition.

She chose a pink Ferrari obviously a special edition model made just for her.

She climbed in and set off.

Mick and Seamus sat in their Police car on the outskirts of Dublin waiting for the usual Saturday night to kick off. It was early and they had just bought two coffees and were enjoying a bit of banter as a pink Ferrari shot past them breaking the speed limit by at least 20k.

Mary sat in the Garda station in her white nightdress; she had failed the breathalyser test. As if the situation could not get any worse, she was suddenly aware that her hands resembled those of a woman of ninety. Her sleek black hair was now as white as snow.

When the officer returned with a glass of wine for the poor old lady who told him her sorry tale, all he could see was a winceyette nightdress lying in the corner of the room. There were a few white parched bones protruding from the sleeves. One of the sleeves had a rather nice Cartier watch hanging from it.

When Mick and Seamus searched Mary's handbag they were amazed to find a copy of Mary's Will the whole of her fortune had been left to a place called 'The

Black Cat's Rest Home.' Later that night they were called to investigate a fire at a mansion in Blackrock. It turned out to be a very unusual case as it appeared that whilst enjoying a Brandy the couple who lived there Niall and Eilish O'Brian, had spontaneously combusted.

Later over a glass of Guinness at Corrigan's bar the men bemoaned the perils of alcohol.

Waiting for Albert?

Doctor Sara Collins looked at her watch if she was lucky she could be home and in bed within the hour. It was one of the few advantages of living in staff accommodation. She sipped her black coffee, yawned and longed for her single bed. She needed to catch up on her sleep if she was going to enjoy her time with John this weekend; they had important things to discuss. Her bleep went, 'Oh damn, here goes my chance to leave on time.' She went to the 'phone and dialled the extension, she knew it was Miller, a care of the elderly ward that wanted her.

'Doctor Collins here, you bleeped me.'

Sister Kate O'Farrell answered, her calm tones confirmed that she was wanted, a lady had developed breathing difficulties and her family who were at her bedside were very concerned. Reading between the lines, Sara could tell that Sister O'Farrell was responding to the family's panicked pleas for a doctor and that Sister would have done everything possible to alleviate the woman's difficulties.

When she arrived on Miller Ward Sister O'Farrell was waiting anxiously and suggested they talk in confidence in her office.

'This is a strange one Sara, no mistake.'

Sara yawned and felt in no mood for anything strange.

'What's the problem Kate, can I see the notes?'

'Sit down first Sara, you don't look too good yourself! I'm going to tell you exactly what they told me.'

'But the patient shouldn't I?'

'I think you really need to hear this first. The lady is called Miss Peters, Alice Peters, she's 105, and the oldest patient we have ever had on this ward. Her relatives are adamant that she must not die tonight, because if she does, she will never be reunited with Albert.'

'I take it that Albert is dead? Is this some sort of rendezvous in the afterlife?'

'Yes I know it sounds crazy, but they are adamant.'

'How do they know all this?'

'They won't tell me, but they sound so convincing.'

'Ok I'll go and speak to them what are their names? And how is the patient?'

'I only know them as Alfred and Ethel, her breathing is laboured but she is as stable as anyone of 105 could be.'

Doctor Collins knocked on Miss Peters' door a frail voice called 'come in'

Miss Peters lay on the bed she was alone and looked as frail as her voice. Sara noticed that her upper chest was moving rapidly; as far as she was concerned it looked like the old lady's body was finally giving out on her. As she approached the bed Miss Peters was able to focus on her face and she gave Sara a most beautiful smile.

'Hello Doctor have you come to pronounce me dead?'

'Not yet Miss Peters, how do you feel?'

'Like I must be dying this time, I've had so many false alarms.'

'Your family are concerned, where are your relatives?'

Not a soul in the world my dear, I managed to outlive them all.'

Sara wrote 'confused' in the lady's notes.

'I am going to listen to your chest now Miss Peters.'

'Do you have children Doctor?'

'No, I am not married.'

'That doesn't concern people these days.'

'I don't get much time for romance, now a nice deep breath for me.'

Sara thought about John, lately he had been busier than her. He had even cancelled his visit last weekend it seemed lately than when she was not working she spent her time waiting for John to call. She had some impor-tant news for him that could not wait too long.

'Then you must make time. I've had all the time in the world and had nothing worth doing with it, time has let me down. Waiting all these years for Albert and he never came.'

Sara looked at the old lady as she checked her pulse. A pair of youthful eyes stared back; it was just possible if she concentrated on the eyes to forget this was a lady of 105.

'Could you pass me the photograph dear.'

Sara passed her the rather tarnished silver frame, which contained a very old photograph. Miss Peters smiled, 'that's me sitting there, I was 19, and I am waiting for someone who never turned up.'

'Was it someone important to you?'

'I thought so at the time, he said he would marry me.'

'Did you ever see him again?'

'No, he joined up and was killed on the first day of the battle of the Somme.'

Sara looked at the photograph it showed a girl in a long dress wearing at hat sitting on a bench outside St Olaf's church.

'Why didn't he want to meet up with a lovely girl like you?'

'He was ambitious and he didn't want to be burdened with a girl like me, I had no prospects I was just a milliner's assistant. He was very good-looking; he had his eye on the boss's daughter. She had her eye on him.'

'How do you know all this?'

'She took the photograph of me and then gave me his note.'

'I didn't think many people had cameras then.'

'You do if your father is a photographer. Her father had 6 shops; he specialised in society portraits. The next time I saw her she gave me this photograph and told me that Albert had proposed to her. She did not live long herself, died of influenza just after the war. Sometimes, I think they gave me their extra years as penance for their guilt.'

'It sounds like a sad time in your life Miss Peters, I would have destroyed it.'

'No it's all I have left to remind me that I was young

and foolish once. I like to look at the photograph and imagine what might have happened if he had turned up. I have had a lot of time to live that life, even if it is only in my imagination.'

Sara left Miss Peters but her words haunted her 'time has let me down' 'He was ambitious' 'you must make time'. Sister O'Farrell was waiting for her at the nursing station.

'Well what do you think Doctor will she meet Albert or miss him by a day?'

'I don't think she wants to meet Albert. Albert let her down. She could go at any time.'

'Were the relatives difficult?'

'They weren't even there; tell them there is no medical intervention required she is as comfortable as she is going to be. I'll look in on her tomorrow afternoon.'

Sara called John when she got off duty.

'I need to know John is there someone else?'

'No not someone, something.'

'What do you mean?'

'It's your ambition Sara, you have no time for me and all that you used to say you wanted, a home and a family.'

Sara laughed.

'John, we have to speak, will you meet me tomorrow afternoon?'

'Why what's happened, you didn't fail some exams did you?'

'No this is more important than exams.'

'Ok I can be there around 4.15.'

'Listen I know this sounds silly, but can we meet somewhere different?'

'Sara are you alright? Yes ok where?'

'Outside St Olaf's Church.'

The next afternoon Sara went to check on Miss Peters finding no one at the nursing station she went straight to Miss Peters' room. It was empty; a middle-aged woman was removing things from the bedside locker.

'Are you a relative of Miss Peters?'

The woman looked at Sara and replied.

'No I am Madge from the nursing home; I am just removing Miss Peters' things although I don't know what we will do with them.'

'What time did she die?'

'This morning at 11.30 am on the dot, it was like she had an appointment.'

'Were her relatives with her?'

'Who?'

'The lady and gentlemen who were here yesterday?'

'No but an elderly gentleman did visit her, according to Sister he was American and said he was a relative. Funny cos she had no family or friends that we knew about, although she did get a letter, here it is, it came from America, I was going to read it to her. Not that she would understand it.'

'But why ever not? She was perfectly able; I had a wonderful conversation with her yesterday. She was telling me about the photograph the one outside the Church.'

'I think you must have had a long day yesterday Doctor, Miss Peters had a stroke five years ago and has not spoken or understood much since.'

Sara shivered and looked around the room the photograph had been put away, but she knew she had not imagined her conversation.

'Can I open the letter? We may need to inform the sender of her death.'

Sara quickly skim read the letter. The contents added to her feeling that something bizarre had happened.

She read the letter to herself again.

'Dear Miss Peters

I hope this letter does not come as too much of a shock to you. I am Nancy Shapiro the grand daughter of Albert Shapiro. I know you are very elderly, but my father said I should write to you. My father said his father often spoke of being adopted and wished he had known why and who his mother was. Recently my grandfather has been ill and I asked my father if I could check via the Internet for information regarding the adoption. Your name showed up and I understand that you never married and have lived in the same town all your life. At first when I saw your age I thought I was too late, but when I checked I found out you are still alive. An agency has helped me do the rest.

I would be most grateful if you or a carer could call me collect on.."

Sara felt herself blush and hastily explained to Madge that she needed to check on something.

She sat at the nursing station and thought of the significance of all she had discovered. Sister O'Farrell appeared.

'You managed it then.'

'What?'

'Miss Peters' rendezvous with Albert.'

Sara handed her the letter and said. 'Yes in this life, not the next though did you meet him?'

'Meet who? She hasn't had any visitors that I know of?

Sara didn't have time to unravel this mystery, her time was precious Miss Peters had taught her that.

'Kate can I leave you to deal with this then, we should call Nancy and let her know about Miss Peters and ask her how Albert Shapiro is doing? Text me when you have the info please.'

Sara sat on the old metal bench and thought about Alice Peters and how she must have felt sitting on the same bench in 1914. John did not arrive at 4.15. She felt that the old lady had told her the story as a way of warning her, as if she could read her mind. A chill blew around her ankles and after looking at her watch for the last time she stood up and started to walk up the path. Suddenly she could hear footsteps and felt a gentle tap on her shoulder. When she turned round John was standing there. He had not run away, he had been caught in traffic.

She blurted it out despite having rehearsed the words so carefully. She found herself asking him somewhat clumsily, if he had any objections to calling their baby Albert.'

'Funny name for a girl though.' Was his immediate reply as he wrapped his arms around her making it impossible for her to walk away.

'Oh I have girls' names in mind too.'

John smiled at her and held her hands as he said.

'We had better have two then, if you have the time and your career will allow it that is?'

She simply replied. 'We have all the time in this world and probably the next.'

Her phone bleeped and she smiled as she read the text.

'Albert Shapiro died 11.30 am our time today.'

As she walked hand in hand with John she wondered why Angels were always depicted as young and pretty, because who else could Alfred and Ethel have been.

DADDY SNORES

I blame the snoring. I have never heard my father snoring, but it must be really powerful because it makes my mammy cry all the time. Snoring uses your money up too. It stops you going on holiday and it even seems to stop people inviting you to parties and all sorts of things. It makes you puke and get fat. It makes you iron your own shirts and sometimes it makes you get up and leave in the night or not sleep at all. I never thought snoring could be so important. Apart from being noisy, it really does seem to cause disturbances and destroy the peace. It stops people hugging and makes them angry, very sad and ill. It can even make smelly 14 year old brothers cry! Snoring is worse than cancer and no one seems to even be doing anything about it. You get charities raising money for cancer but I've never heard of anyone collecting for a cure for snoring have you?

It seemed to get really bad in December just after my 10th birthday. 3 days after Christmas I found daddy sleeping on the sofa one morning. At first I thought he was sick cos to be honest he didn't look good, but when I asked him what was wrong he told me that Mammy couldn't sleep because he snored so much.

Mammy must have been very tired because she spent the whole of New Years day in bed. I asked my brother what was wrong, but he just grunted and retreated to his bedroom. Granma O'Sullivan came to visit and that seemed to do the trick cos Mammy was out of the bed and sitting in the kitchen drinking tea with her and listening as Granma told her how wonderful her son is and how lucky she is to be married to such a great man. Daddy didn't sleep on the sofa that night, but the moment Granma left, Mammy took to her bed again. Daddy was back to sleeping on the sofa too.

I came home from school a few weeks later to find the house upside down! There was Mike the builder, a friend of my daddy's banging and crashing in the garage at the side of the house. Mammy wasn't home, but Daddy was there wearing his gardening clothes and this bit really shocked me he was smoking! I had never seen my daddy smoke before, he made his own and they were kind of thin and wispy and he sucked at them sort of hungrily. I couldn't help wondering if they would affect the snoring for good or bad.

I asked Daddy what was going on and he was full of talk of a conversion and to be honest I had no idea what he meant, I've heard about Protestants being converted but didn't think this was anything to do with Mike. And when I saw a big hole in the wall between our utility room and the garage I was so pleased that my mammy was out. There was dust everywhere and I knew Mammy doesn't care for dust and muck of any kind. All through January and February the work went on and on. One day I asked Mammy what was going on and she said that Daddy's snoring had got so bad that he would have to move into the garage because she couldn't put up with it any longer. Then she burst into tears and went up to her bedroom

Snoring is not good for you and neither is smoking. And neither is drinking! Mammy has started having her friend Sue come round on a Saturday night. Granma Boyle doesn't think much of Sue, calls her 'the divorced one' and told Mammy last time she was here that spending her Saturday nights drinking with Sue was giving out a very wrong message to all and sundry. I can tell my daddy doesn't like it either cos now he has taken to going out with Mike and leaving Mammy and Sue to 'their own devices' as he puts it.

By March the building work was all finished and then something very strange happened I came home to find a big van parked in our drive and watched as new furniture was being carried in through our back gate through the new back entrance to the house that led to the newly converted garage. Daddy was there, but there was no sign of Mammy. Mrs Rooney next door stood and watched and shook her head with obvious disapproval.

I have to say that Daddy's new room in the garage looks great, he has it painted white with a white carpet and fitted wardrobes and he even has his own bathroom and his own back door. He must be hoping the snoring stops though cos he has this massive iron bed with black satin sheets that match the black towels in his bathroom so there is plenty of room for Mammy. Mammy told him he had to wash his own sheets and things cos she wasn't setting a foot inside his something pad, oh yes his 'sag pad' well it didn't look saggy to me. He's even got a little room built into the garage roof where he has a so-fabed and television and his computer. I think Mammy's jealous really cos Daddy now has the best bedroom in the house. I told Dad his room looked nice and Mammy screamed at him 'And so it should for what it cost!' Daddy just shrugged and started taking all of his clothes out of his wardrobe and moving them to his sag pad.

Daddy hasn't got a phone in his new bedroom and he doesn't know this, but I have taken to listening in when he makes calls. I feel sort of bad for doing it really, but now I just can't seem to help myself. He was telling someone last night that he has to 'grin and bear it' that 8 years will fly by because the last 8 have. He was smiling while he was on the phone and the other person must be funny cos he was laughing a lot.

Mammy was in the other room doing some ironing. She is so jealous of Daddy's new bedroom that she has stopped doing his ironing! He does look sort of funny when he does it and he swears a lot cos he keeps burning his fingers and his shirts. He is really bad at it Mammy just laughs at his crinkled shirts and says it's a shame that they only make the shirts he likes out of cotton.

I was sad this week though, cos my friend Carly and her parents always go on holiday with us every summer over to France. We stay in two big caravans at a great camp site in the Vendee. When I asked Mammy about the trip this summer she sat me down and told me that we wouldn't be going this year. I burst out crying and kept asking why and then she finally told me that there was no money left for holidays because of the building work. Then I asked if Carly could come over to play cos I wanted to show her Daddy's new room. Well Mammy's face went all red when I said that. She went over to the sink and washed up some cutlery and told me that no one was to know about Daddy's new bedroom and especially not Carly and Granma O'Sullivan. When I said that Mrs Rooney next door knew, cos she asked me about the building and the new furniture Mammy ran out of the room and I think she was sick in the toilet!

The next day Carly told me that we were no longer invited to their barbecue party because things would be 'awkward' was the reason her parents had given her. I suppose if Daddy fell asleep after a few drinks like he usually does and stared snoring it would be very embarrassing for Mammy and yes 'awkward.'

My brother really is a horrible person! I try to avoid him but I was so upset about not going to France and I wanted to know if he knew and was upset too. I knocked on his bedroom door and eventually he said 'who's there?'

I said it's me and he told me where to go! So I just opened the door and walked in and that made him really cross. I asked him if he knew about the holiday and he told me to 'f off.'

He knew alright cos he was crying.

Well today something very odd happened Granma O'Sullivan had a stroke and poor Daddy is beside himself, but for once Mammy seems happy! It seems Mammy went to the hospital and has invited her to come and live with us! When I went to see Granma O'Sullivan she

didn't make much sense. She can walk but she can't manage stairs and she can't talk. Well every cloud has a silver
lining as my Mammy said. Daddy asked where Granma
would sleep and Mammy's reply made sense. His bed is
very big and Granma is very deaf and won't hear the
snoring and there's always his sofa bed.

I wonder how long Granma will be living with us?
If bad snoring lasts only 8 years she won't have to share
with Daddy for too long. As Daddy said he will just have
to 'keep grinning and bearing it.'

STATIONS OF LOSS

It was Kate's idea to go and see them. The 14 Stations of the Cross in St John's church in Bethnal Green, for Margaret just the thought of it brought back memories of school, cold chapels, funerals and wet Easters the end of lent and denial. Kate's enthusiasm for these paintings was very contagious. Margaret had brought Kate up in a rather secular manner but something was drawing Kate towards religion. Kate had explained over the phone why they had to see these iconic paintings.

'It took him eight years to complete and he used his son and daughter as models', she gushed and to make sure that Margaret was up in time to be at the church by 10 a.m. she insisted that she stayed the night, her mother was fond of sleeping in at weekends. Margaret went along with it all to please Kate, her daughter seemed determined to educate her.

Margaret wished Kate would be less interested in art and literature and a little more interested in men and babies. Margaret wanted to be a grandmother. She longed for a grandson, but could not bring herself to tell Kate how she felt and why. Kate had been let down by too many young men she didn't waste her time searching for Prince Charming when all she seemed to meet was frogs. Especially, the ones that never turned into princes, however many times you kissed them.

Neither of them was prepared for what happened next.

St John's church was unremarkable, but when Margaret looked at the man representing Jesus in the painting, something strange happened. As Margaret stared at him, his eyes seemed to see right through her and the Virgin Mary's tears seemed oh so familiar. Margaret walked through the church in a trance as if she was 10 years old again; the year her beloved brother died. She hadn't realised it until she looked at the paintings of the Stations of the Cross, that she had pictures in her mind, sketchy drawings of events that led up to her brother's death. She had never spoken much about her brother to her children. Kate and her sister had been part of her healing, and she never wanted to burden them with any of her sorrow.

Now she went to a different part of the church unable to tell Kate what effect these paintings were having on her.

Her children were unaware of how when they passed the age at which her brother had died, she had sighed with relief, and with every year they survived she felt more blessed. Her mother was dead now, but when she looked at the Virgin Mary's tears she knew she had seen them in real life many, many times.

'Are you alright madam?'

A tall man with piercing blue eyes was looking at her, he reminded her of someone and just this little act of kindness was too much for her to bear.

'No I don't believe I am. It's these paintings they are bringing back such painful memories.'

The man led her to a pew near the door and offered her a tissue from a packet which he kept in the inside pocket of his coat. The tears were streaming down her face, tears for a time long ago. Her brother would have been 50 this year, she told the man that her brother had been dead 35 years, 'forever 15', was the phrase we used, forever frozen in adolescence and my memories of his death are frozen images like these paintings. The man nodded and listened and Margaret talked.

I. Patrick gets an invitation to a beach party.

My mother wished that she had forbidden him to go, but that wasn't her style and she trusted people to look after her children as if they were their own. I still have the invitation.

II. Patrick says goodbye to his family.

I was going to stay with my friend Lottie for a week and before I left I went into Patrick's bedroom and woke him up and gave him a big hug. I thought he might be cross that I woke him, but he cuddled me and told me to behave myself. I wasn't an easy child and my parents were going through a divorce, this brought me and Patrick closer together. When our Dad told us he was moving out Patrick and I were re- lieved, we were fed up with the rows.

III. Patrick is missing.

My Dad came home to find a note pinned to the back

door, 'Please contact Police Sergeant Grimes on....' It was the day after the party and it was 1 pm by the time they worked out Patrick was missing. Last sighted at 4 am

Four days they sat waiting for him to be found. His friends made one of those appeals on local TV it was even mentioned on Radio 4.

I didn't know Patrick was missing, I was protected. I do remember being cross when I was told that all of the televisions at my friend's house were broken. Then we were taken to a cottage in the middle of nowhere where there weren't any televisions or people. It was on the news and in the papers and I was oblivious to it all. I rang home every day and my mum must have made a Herculean effort to sound normal even when I asked to speak to Patrick her voice gave nothing away.

Four days sitting in the kitchen with the vicar and the family liaison officers the curtains closed to avoid people snooping. The bins were locked up to avoid the press searching for snippets of information, desperately keen for scandal. The press asked people in the local pub for any juicy tit bits that might put the family in the frame. Nothing was forthcoming. Friends descended to care for my mother I was so pleased when I heard that and saw them holding my mother up, they were her emotional crutches.

IV. Patrick is dead.

The day I was due to go home Lottie's mummy told me there had been a change of plans my mum and dad were coming to collect me from Lottie's house the next day. We drove to Lottie's house and found that all of the televisions were still broken. The next day I packed all my stuff and waited for my parents to arrive. They arrived in my mum's car which seemed odd at the time. Lottie's mum opened the door and hugged my mum and dad in turn and then she seemed to disappear leaving me with my parents who both looked as though they had shrunk since I saw them last, my mum had hollow cheeks and my dad had dark sockets for eyes. They took me through to the sitting room in silence and do you know I knew there had been a death, I could smell death not that I even knew what that smell was and I thought my dog had been run over she was only a puppy and had no road sense.

My mum did all of the talking and the words 'Patrick has died' burnt into my consciousness like a red hot poker through my core causing me pain, real physical pain. My soul mate, the only person in the world who understood what it was like to be in our family was dead. I don't remember but my mother told me the first thing I said was 'poor, poor Patrick and now I am an only child.' My mum told me she had kept all the newspapers and one day I may want to read what happened and then I understood why none of the televisions worked and why we had driven in the dark to the cottage in the forest. I must have been a strange little girl because on the way home we stopped at a service station and I insisted on having a clock work hamster toy which was dressed as the 'grim reaper' and when you wound the key it waved its scythe demonically. Patrick would have loved that!

V. Patrick's soul is commended to God.

Patrick did come home again, but I couldn't see him because he was lying in his coffin. He was placed in the sitting room and we carried on around him. The house stank of lillies, one smell of a sickly sweet Lily and I am back there again watching my mother place big church candles on my brother's coffin. Granma, Auntie Mary and mum's best friend Maureen had held a sort of wake in the kitchen the night before the funeral. Dad wasn't around he had already moved out. Patrick's coffin was cool it was spray painted silver and had the name of his favourite band written down the side. He had a rock star funeral with his favourite music and everyone wearing their normal clothes and anything that they wanted to wear, some dyed their hair and played their electric guitars in the church. The lyrics were screened though. We all said our pieces about Patrick even me. He would have loved it. After the funeral just his closest family went to the crematorium and that was the saddest bit, watching his cool coffin disappear.

VI. Patrick's last party

We had a marquee in the garden and his friends drank beer and we ate pizza and hotdogs. The photos show us having a good time, like he liked to do. They don't show me sleeping in my mum's bed, or mum and I bracing ourselves for all those 'firsts' first day back at school without Patrick etc. I used to go into Patrick's room we left it like it was the day we went to the party for a long time. I could smell him so strongly in there, I never thought about it when he was alive but once he had gone it was overwhelming a mixture of deodorant and his smelly feet. At his funeral party mum displayed ring binders that contained things from the different stages of his life for everyone to look at and there were big baskets of his stuff for each stage from baby toys to CD's. His things outlived him I still have some of his things, his watch, some of his exercise books and all of those ring binders with his swimming certificates and his detention slips. Patrick was no saint.

VII. Patrick's inquest

My parents kept quiet about this and I didn't attend. His friends were witnesses and they told it like it was. The coroner concluded that it was accidental death but said it was a miracle that there were not more fatalities because the combination of a hot sunny day, alcohol and a river and the sea were a disaster waiting to happen. What he failed to say was that there was a lack of adult supervision that these young people were left to fend for themselves whilst the adults were at home having a barbecue and no doubt getting drunk too. Patrick was let down, he had been drinking heavily and had been sick he was last seen at 4 am asleep not one single adult had thought to take him to the house to be kept an eye on, he was left to camp on the beach with only another 15 year old to take care of him. In the morning there was no sign of him. No one will ever really know what happened; did he think he should go for a swim? Did he go for a walk and fall into the river? No one knows because he was alone. I used to wonder if he was aware that he was going to drown, did he fall in and struggle, or was he too drunk to know? What were his last thoughts? For four days his body drifted until someone found it, I often wonder about that person and how they coped after that grim discovery.

VIII. Patrick's ashes

My mother collected Patrick's ashes, not much to show really all that was left of the body that we knew so well and was still growing. We will never know if Patrick would have become the 6ft guy he so wanted to be. When no one was around I used to unscrew the plastic urn and look at his ashes which were really his ground up bones mixed with the bits left over of his coffin. I could see specs of silver dust. I stole some of them and used to keep them in an old perfume bottle, mum threw it out one day not realising what or who was in it. His ashes went on a proper tour, some were put in a rocket on bonfire night and set off over our garden, others were scattered in his favourite park. On the day of judgement Patrick will have a hard time reconstituting his old body! It does upset me that there is no grave to visit just places that played a part in his life and death.

IX. Patrick is still my brother.

Children can be so cruel; when I went back to school some children taunted me and told me my brother was a drunk. I hated people who didn't know me asking me if I had any brothers or sisters. Mum told me that it didn't matter what anyone said, what happened to Patrick could happen to anyone even the Prime Minister's son was found drunk in Leicester Square and Prince Harry was always getting drunk. She told me that no one could take my memories away and for ten years I had a brother and his legacy is the love we have for him even though he is not with us.

X. Patrick's friends remember him.

Every year on the anniversary of Patrick's death his friends remember him. They made this vow and have kept to it. They return to the beach and make a camp fire and play his favourite music. Over the years as his friends got older they brought girlfriends and then wives and children. The older they got the angrier they became, when they realised that leaving 15 year olds on a beach with a shed load of alcohol was as irresponsible as letting a toddler play with a loaded gun.

XI. Patrick should not be forgotten.

We that were left behind had to carry on with our lives, and mum and I did just that. Dad found someone new, and after a while he seemed to prefer his new partner and her son to me. Mum never re married and died in her bed very suddenly the way she wanted to at the age of 75. I got married young and had Kate and Sara. Kate's dad and I are still friends, but I don't think any man I met was as good to me as my brother was, or was a patch on him. I wasn't allowed to talk about my brother in front of the children, my husband said it was bad luck and morbid.

XII. Patrick lives on in me.

As I grew older I realised that Patrick lived on in me and I needed to make the most of my life I owed that to him. I used to do things and go places that I thought he would have wanted to do. He was a shadow in my life always there, but do you know I feel guilty because I should have told Kate or Sara about my brother. I didn't want to scare them.

The tall man nodded and Margaret realised that Kate was sitting next to him. There were tears in her eyes, she reached out and held her mother's hands.

XIII. Patrick meets his future mother-in-law.

'Mum, this is Patrick, you seem to have found each other, and he is the kind of man who everyone confides in. One of the reasons for getting you here was to meet Patrick, Mum. Patrick is a vicar and I wanted you to meet him and see his favourite church. I know you have been hoping that I would meet someone, but all of the men of my age just didn't seem right. I was scared of telling you that I was in love with a man who is much older than me. But I think having met him now you will know what I see in him. Mum, Patrick and I are engaged and if you like this church and you obviously like Patrick. This is where we want to be married.'

Margaret smiled and looked deep into Patrick's eyes and something made her ask.

'When is your birthday'

'He smiled and confirmed that he was born on 1st August'

XIV. Patrick lives on in those who loved him.

Margaret smiled and for the first time in years she felt truly happy. She didn't think Patrick would believe in reincarnation but how did he get those beautiful eyes? Her brother Patrick was no longer a secret either, and now she felt she would be able to share her brother with others. The stages of loss are many and time does not truly heal. Time is relative and Patrick's brief life was no less important than any other's. Age fades away when we look deep into a person's eyes, the windows to the soul. Age is nothing; it is just the passing of each year for those who are lucky enough to survive.

A FAMILIAR STRANGER

By

GERRY ROSE

I have included the synopsis prologue and first three chapters of my first novel.

SYNOPSIS

'Familiar stranger' spans the years 1916-1999. It combines a story of growing up Irish in England with the story of Bridget Collins, an Irish woman who like many others had no choice but to leave Ireland in 1938 to find work in England. The novel can be viewed partly as a family saga. Bridget's eldest daughter Bernadette chose to cut herself off from her family in 1974. Bridget living on her own in Essex a place she loathes, spends a lot of her time dwelling on the past, about the reasons she left Ireland and looking for clues in Bernadette's childhood as to why she chose to reject her family. Bridget's 3 remaining daughters are 3 very different women they feel they have suffered because of Bernadette's decision.

Bernadette may have good reasons for her action, her experiences of returning from Ireland aged 2 to meet a father she had never met were traumatic. The family were subject to 'No blacks, no Irish' prejudice which was prevalent at this time. This made housing difficult, so they were forced together with many other families to squat in an old army base in Essex in the post war period which seemed to drag on as 'homes fit for heroes' became less of a priority.

Whilst much of the novel focuses on Bridget's loss of her daughter, it also examines the reasons why Bernadette took such a drastic action but it also shows how this has affected the lives of her sisters.

Maureen had a very difficult relationship with Bernadette and once Bernadette had vowed never to return, Maureen renamed herself Christina and felt able to be the person she had been prevented from becoming whilst Bernadette was around.

Fran, always in the shadow of Bernadette but also subject to her bullying feels happy with the status quo.

Angela Collins the youngest daughter is perhaps the only one with happy fond memories of the beautiful Bernadette.

Whilst for years the family struggle to deal with the fact that Bernadette has disowned them and some of them have dealt with it, suddenly this is altered by a phone call from Clara, Bernadette's daughter.

The news Clara has to impart throws the Collins family into a situation where the past has to be confronted. Bernadette has a degenerative disease and perhaps some of her behaviour can be explained, as possible early signs of the disease.

The family have to unite to confront the reality of this dreadful disease and to support their niece. But what if this reveals a secret in the family?

What if Bridget is forced to confront the truth about her past?

The novel is far from being completely dark, Bridget Collins is a quick witted woman who possesses a silver tongue for the 'put down'. The Collins family are survivors who would never have described themselves as close but who never the less learn that families can contain all the evils of the world, and yet despite this are the best training ground for learning to deal with them.

FAMILIAR STRANGER

Prologue

January 1999

I thought I saw Bernadette again today, I was doing my weekly shopping in what's left of the shops in the town and I saw this pretty girl come walking towards me. I felt my stomach flip over, she stood out, - rather stylish for Fairfleet, with her navy suit, high heels and blonde hair. I thought she must have just come off the London train. She was slim and had the face of an Angel- the heads turned all right. When she smiled my heart did a little jig. A group of boys whistled as she passed by and she turned her head and laughed. She had good legs and that touch of glamour in her walk; she even smiled at me when she noticed I was watching her. Then all of a sudden I remembered that I had to get to the post office before it shut, but when I searched in my bag for my pension book it wasn't there. I panicked a bit, convinced someone must have taken it from my bag. When I looked up, there she was, standing in front of me and smiling.

Bernadette always had a smile that could melt you, no matter what she'd done or said. I looked into her eyes and a voice inside me struggled to make itself heard.

Bernadette, Bernadette come on now, come home with me, it's like feeding strawberries to pigs, you're wasting yourself on this lot.

And then she spoke.
'You all right darlin?'

The illusion was shattered, I wasn't her darlin! The Essex accent I have always hated. To think people still say my Irish accent is hard to understand. This girl's words fell lazily from her loose, painted, lips. Close up I could see her dark roots and the bad cut of her suit. She smelled of cheap perfume and cigarette smoke. Sure then it hit me, she was about twenty-two and my Bernadette would be in her fifties now. At least the girl must have been well brought up to be bothered with an old lady. That's all I ever wanted people to say about my Bernadette. That's not what she thought and maybe she's right, because I haven't seen her for twenty-five years and I'll probably never see her again. She could even be long dead for all I know.

My other daughters tell me that you even find rejects in a batch of biscuits made out of the same dough and baked in the same oven and that three out of four isn't bad. But your first born is always special. Still my other girls try their best, but when I'm alone, which I am a lot since Frank died; I sit and think about Bernadette. To me she is still the most loving of my children.

I often imagine what my life would have been like, if I had never come back to England with Bernadette. It's too late for regrets now and soon I'll be past caring. On long dark evenings I sit and think. My thoughts are mine to think and all I nurse now is my memories.

CHAPTER 1

Christina woke up and felt the same thoughts that had nagged at her before she had drifted off to sleep, slowly return. At first it was just a sensation something you could not even describe, but Christina knew that something was not right. For the last few weeks she had had the strange notion that she was being watched. At first she had dismissed this as being yet another tiresome symptom of the menopause. She was developing a kind of paranoia. She felt sure that the man she had seen waiting at the bus stop near her home, had been the same man who had held the door open for her at the office yesterday. These were things she could not even begin to tell Giles about. Giles would pat her hand and laugh. He would probably delight in telling her that he had been warning her about 'over working,' that at her age she should be slowing down. Good old Giles, had taken to early retirement so well, despite everyone's fears that he would miss the power and status of his role as senior partner.

Giles was fast asleep, his balding head snuggled deep in the pillow, made her think of a helpless baby, so still, so vulnerable. But as Giles snorted and let out a long rattling snore, all thoughts of babies shot from her mind. Giles always smiled as he slept a testament to the contentment he felt with his life. Christina envied him, he had a clear conscience and had to date, led a faultless, if a little dull, dutiful life. Christina was also aware that she was part of the reason for his contentment. The last twenty-four years of her life had been lived with a man who adored her. Or at least he adored what she allowed him to know of her.

She entered the shower and took refuge in its power to cleanse and invigorate. A while later swathed in a large fluffy white bath sheet, she found herself choosing a simple, clean-cut, black, trouser suit with a plain blouse. Today she longed to be invisible.

She opened her bedroom curtains and looked down at the street below. Luckily, she had managed to park her car very near to the front door last night. She would drive to the office today, she needed to feel safe. Anyone who was following her would be more obvious, she could watch in her mirror, no one would be able to follow her from Pimlico to Knightsbridge unnoticed. She would take a detour then she would know. She was shaking as she fumbled for her car keys. Once she was in the street she stood still for a moment, her legs felt frail as they teetered on high stiletto shoes, before walking down the steps. As usual her street was quiet, it had been what had attracted her and Giles when they had first viewed the apartment. The illusion of peace in the centre of London and yet only a stone's throw from the tube.

The man who delivered the letter no longer needed to watch Christina, all had been confirmed and now his job was over.

Giles collected the post later, which as usual was to be found trapped in the basket attached to the letter box on the front door. He felt amused by his new found role as post boy to the apartments. It was all part of retirement really; doing jobs that others had done for you for years. Giles peered at the handwritten envelope and puzzled over it for a few minutes, before placing it on the table together with a new set of take away pizza flyers. He posted the letters for the other tenants in their pigeon holes and carried his post together with Christina's considerably bigger bundle back to the apartment.

The letter addressed to 'Maureen Collins' in an almost childlike script was still lying on the hall table when Christina returned to the apartment. She had a habit of checking the table for stray letters. Occasionally a letter would arrive for Saskia and she would dutifully take it back to her apartment to readdress it to her friend and ex neighbour who had moved back to Amsterdam. She felt her heart leap uncomfortably as she read the name on the envelope. She felt paralysed, her stomach felt as if it had been grasped by a steel hand which twisted it until she felt she might faint with the pain. However her mind raced ahead in an almost methodical way, regardless. Who would write to her here using this name? She knew without having to calculate that it was twenty-five years since she had used the name Maureen. Even her mother had finally got used to calling her Christina. There was only one person who would still think of her as being Maureen. But how would Bernadette have traced her, after all these years? Could Bernadette be watching her? The answer would be found in the envelope but Christina did not even want to touch it, let alone open it. If even the envelope seemed poisonous, reading the contents of any letter it contained would be the equivalent of opening Pandora's Box. Once she had made the decision it was as though the paralysis had been lifted and Christina walked away from the table leaving the letter untouched. Her pace quickened as she got nearer to her apartment she panicked as she searched for the key. She knew that if she did not get inside her apartment within the next few seconds she would vomit on the pale beige carpet she had so vehemently fought for, over a hotel style red patterned one when the 'common parts' had been redecorated a year ago.

Back in her apartment the feeling of nausea subsided and her logical side took over. She had left the envelope on the table where it would remain indefinitely with the usual pile of takeaway menus and business cards advertising mini cab companies, until someone used some initiative and disposed of it. But she imagined that Bernadette would know if she claimed it, she was trying to catch her out. A cold shiver walked slowly down her spine. She had no desire to read the letter there was nothing anyone had to say to Maureen that would interest Christina. They were two different people separated by a time when she had lived in another's shadow.

When she had calmed down she went out ignoring the envelope which sat unclaimed in the hall. Two days later when she left for work she noticed that the letter had disappeared together with the unwanted leaflets. Giles had not mentioned the letter, so at first she did not say anything about it, or the fact that whenever she was alone the telephone would ring, but whoever rang never left a message on their answer phone and the number was always 'withheld'. She found herself distracted at work and when a client rang up to complain that she had missed an important meeting that she had made with them directly, she knew she was allowing her fears to interfere with her business. Christina decided it was time to tell Giles a few home truths- not everything of course, but enough so he could be of some support to her. She would have to warn Giles that Bernadette was about to re enter her life and spoil all that she had worked so hard to create.

She left work earlier than usual and drove to the Fulham road. Giles was an easy man to please. His love of Italian olives, cheese, wine and fresh pasta would be easily satisfied by visiting his favourite shop. She parked in the Chelsea and Westminster Hospital's underground car park it was more expensive than finding a meter. She felt sure the health service would put the money to better use than the local council. She passed a group of patients attached to drips who stood by the revolving door dragging deeply on their cigarettes. The chill of the late September day would not be good for them, but they looked as though they had far greater concerns than a mild autumn breeze. She was reminded of the days when she used to smoke, just one of a series of things that Bernadette had introduced her to-all bad of course.

Back at the apartment Christina unpacked her purchases with the excitement of knowing that Giles would think Christmas, New Year and Easter had arrived on the same day. He was easily pleased but she was aware that she had probably spent more on this one meal for two than her mother ever spent on a week's family shopping. She could imagine what her mother would say if she was here now. Well she wasn't here or likely to be invited back after the rude comments she had made about the apartment.

'Sure it's very white. Don't things get dirty quickly? All this white is sure to do your eyesight no good.'

Christina opened the first bottle of Chianti, she had been careful to choose labels she recognised, they had spent enough time in Tuscany over the last few years for Giles to be on first name terms with many of the growers in the Classico region. The wine's bouquet reminded her of those lazy sunny days lying by the pool, sun kissed and comfortable in Giles' undemanding presence. She put the olives, caramelised onions and artichoke hearts into white bowls and wrapped the olive and anchovy focaccia in foil, ready to be warmed in the oven, then she grated the parmigiano reggiano. It was to be a simple meal- the way Giles liked things, uncomplicated but containing the best ingredients. The pappardelle with mixed wild mushrooms was simple to prepare. They would have plenty of time to talk. She unwrapped the special cheeses which Giles much preferred to dessert, he would be particularly pleased that she managed to get some of his favourite ricotta.

She had just finished laying the table when Giles arrived. She heard him come in immediately stow his squash racket in the hall cupboard and empty his sports bag into the laundry basket in the utility room.

'Mmm something smells delicious! Are you spoiling me?'

Giles entered looking relaxed and clean after his game of squash and sauna. Christina kissed his cheek and breathed in the heady scent of his aftershave. Giles was a man whose looks had improved with age, maturity had added distinction to his bland features, just as it had robbed some of his contemporaries of their clean good looks which had been based on sexy eyes and blonde hair. Giles approved of the wine and poured them both a large glass. They rarely drank during the week and Giles smiled to himself and felt a stirring which he felt sure predicted a night of love making. He had learned to accept over the years that he must allow Christina to take the initiative in their sex life. Although it didn't happen very often he knew that when it did he was rarely disappointed. They sometimes went months without making love, only to have this followed by months when Christina seemed insatiable. He had never discovered why this should be, but he just felt grateful that after twenty-four years of making love to the same woman, he could feel the way he did tonight, just imagining the night ahead.

They sat on the matching white sofas opposite each other, holding their glasses carefully both not wanting to spill any wine on the pristine covers. Silences between them were usually quite comfortable. Christina's outer calm belied her inner struggle to find the right words to explain her fears. Giles always hated long winded stories and explanations, she would have to be brief and concise

if she was going to keep his attention and convince him
that he should take her seriously.

'Giles, have you ever regretted that we never had
children?'

Giles gave her one of his looks which she knew meant-
'Oh you want to talk serious stuff.'

'Christina what has brought this on? We haven't had
this conversation for a few years now.'

There had been a time early on in their relationship
when they had even toyed with the idea of letting nature
take its course. Christina had been careful not to leave
such things to something as messy and unpredictable as
nature.

'Oh just thinking about families in general, Giles.'

'Have your sisters been on the 'phone again? I suppose it's getting near to the annual pilgrimage to visit
your mother. Will you go with them this year? You
ought to she's getting on a bit you know.'

'I know, but no, they haven't. Well at least Angela
and Frances haven't. But I have felt for the last few weeks
now that I am being watched.'

Giles stared at her and with a look of quiet consterna-
tion said, 'absolute nonsense. Is dinner ready?'

'It will only take a few minutes. I'm being serious you
know, I feel as if I'm being watched.'

'I think you've being watching too many James Bond
repeats on the box, Chrissy.'

Christina felt patronised and knew that Giles only had
eyes and mind for food tonight. And if he thought she

was going to oblige his other fantasies he was going to be disappointed.

They sat at the table and shared out the artichokes, caramelised onions and olives. Giles cut chunks of bread marvelling at its freshness. He told Christina about his squash game in minute detail, unaware and unconcerned that she was obviously not paying attention to a single word. Christina had little appetite, the strongly smelling onions seemed to compete with the aroma of the artichokes making the earlier feeling of nausea return. She nibbled at a small piece of bread having carefully removed the olives and anchovies first. The pasta left Giles speechless and Christina was too deep in thought to notice or care.

Later having cleared up Christina left Giles to watch the news. She was asleep or at least gave every illusion of being asleep by the time Giles came to bed.

Christina waited until Giles left the apartment on Saturday morning and waited and watched as he loaded his golf clubs into the boot of his Jaguar.

Dear Giles she thought, so predictable so reliable. She waited ten minutes before going upstairs and raising the loft hatch, retrieving the retractable ladder and climbing up into the loft space. She flicked on the light and grimaced as she saw the cobwebs that lay like a fine silk mesh over the old suitcases and boxes that were piled up on either side of the hatch. There was the faint aroma of cypress and she remembered that Giles had gone to a lot of trouble storing his father's old army uniform in special moth proof bags, whilst she had thrown things into boxes and suitcases with little care whether they survived, but not brave enough to throw them away.

She sat on the floor in the space between their respective piles of property. She reached for a box that Giles had neatly labelled 'Photographs-babyhood up to starting secondary school 1942-1953. Inside she found leather bound albums of black and white photographs attached to the pages by silver photographs corners. A neat hand had annotated them, 'Giles, Crystal Palace aged two', 'Giles, Brighton beach 1947', 'Giles, first day Croydon Grammar.' There were photos of the family taken at the zoo and birthdays and Christmas which featured smiling aunts and bespectacled cousins. The stuff of most people's lives, some may even say a record of a rather ordinary, mundane life. She carefully replaced the albums and closed the box.

She had to search through a succession of her boxes containing work papers, cuttings and invoices before she found an old manila envelope that contained her past. She poured its contents onto the floor in front of her and felt her chest tighten as the dust rose and the memories replayed.

One rather creased photograph stood out. It was of her and Bernadette standing outside what was their first home-Meesons Camp. She shuddered, but looked closely at the photograph hoping that it would reveal something to show her that what had happened was predictable. The photograph showed an attractive girl, of about eleven with blonde curly hair and big eyes. She was looking directly at the camera with her arms around her younger, plainer sister in what looked like an embrace. On closer inspection and in Christina's heart she knew that in reality, she Maureen, as she was then was being restrained, not hugged.

Another was a family photo taken at the new house, the date scribbled in pencil on the back said 1956. It showed Bernadette a sultry teenager draped on the arm of one end of the sofa, whilst she sat wedged between her parents, looking timid next to a beaming toddler-Frances and baby Angela sitting on her mother's knee smiling a big gummy smile. She remembers that divan sofa, part of a three piece suite bought on hire purchase. To her ten year old's eye the red 'bobbly' fabric had at first given the room a majestic feel, but her mother had spoiled that by covering it in antimacassars which had masses of sprigged shamrocks embroidered on them. Her mother had said the sofa was designed to be used as a guest bed. The thought of guests sounded exotic and exciting but none ever came and this had felt like a betrayal even then.

She looked closer as if it could reveal answers to the questions that flew around her head. She had no memory of posing for this photograph, yet the photograph proved that the event took place. Christina stared at Bernadette and felt stricken again by a deep seated feeling of panic, she must not let this person enter her life again. She scooped up the photographs and put them back into the envelope. She wished she could throw it away, but she still found its contents both repelling and fascinating. The telephone rang and she decided to let it go on to answer phone. As she climbed down the ladder she heard part of the message that was being recorded.

'I wish to speak to Maureen Collins most urgently please...'

Christina froze on the ladder her hands gripped the sides so tightly that her knuckles went very white. Her legs shook involuntarily and her mouth felt suddenly dry. She didn't recognise the voice but felt sure it had something to do with Bernadette. Her hands gripped the ladder, and she felt the same paralysis that she had experienced in the hall yesterday. She was aware of what she was doing, but was powerless to control it. She felt like she was in a deep, water filled quarry and the ladder was her only means of escape. But she could not move and she knew that soon the water would rise and drown her.

CHAPTER 2

Frances put the 'phone down and sighed heavily. She walked into the kitchen ignoring the abandoned bowls of breakfast cereal. She opened the fridge but could not ignore the photograph that she had stuck on the front of it. It was a truly repulsive image, it showed her in her bathing suit in the pool with Celeste on their summer holiday last year. She didn't know why the photograph had triggered the desire to diet, she often felt she had been born fat, but the few baby photographs that she had seen did not support this theory. She often wondered if she had had no choice but to become fat.

The salad box bulged with celery, lettuce, cucumber and tomatoes. She grimaced and shut the door, she kept her eyes closed as she felt for the cupboard and only opened them when she felt confident that the next thing she would see was chocolate.

She had always loved chocolate. Her happiest childhood memories always contained a bar of the new Galaxy chocolate or a box of Maltesers. Bernadette and chocolate would be forever linked in her memory. She remembered John Whitaker one of Bernadette's first conquests, he'd lived in a detached house on the road that Bernadette and Maureen, as she was then, had walked along on their way to the Convent School. She had told

Frances that one morning he had stood by his front gate and called out to them as they passed. He had said that he was doing Art A' level and wanted to draw Bernadette. Things like that were always happening to Bernadette. Maureen had gone along with her the first few times so Mammy and Daddy would not get suspicious. But one day Maureen refused and Bernadette said she had to come. When Bernadette said you had to do something you did it —or else. She thought about that time a lot, a time when Bernadette was such a large part of their lives. It must have been around 1959, she would have been about six or seven. It seemed like only yesterday, still so vivid, so real. Sitting in the bedroom that Bernadette shared with Maureen watching her get dressed.

'As soon as I'm dressed we'll be off Frances. You're not going to be naughty today are you?'

'Where we going then?'

'Our little secret- you like chocolate now don't you.'

'Course, everyone in the whole wide world likes chocolate.'

'Course they do and it's not often they see the bar you're going to get.'

'Yippee. Why are you doing that?'

'Oh I'm making Hairy Mary smell beautiful.'

'I don't have hairs there.'

'Not at the moment but one day you will.'

'And then I'll have to puts perfume on them too.'

Frances remembered walking up the road proud to be

with her glamorous sister. Bernadette, blonde, slim and of course what she recognised now —sexy. Her mother of course couldn't handle it. To anyone born in Ireland when the Church was still so powerful, sex was the dirtiest word of them all. Her mother didn't know the half of it. And her father? He must have had a good idea of what she got up to. He used to follow them all. She remembered seeing him on his bike watching her from the road, whilst she played with friends at the recreation ground. No one had the power to stop Bernadette from being herself.

John Whittaker lived in the kind of house that their mother would have loved. Not ostentatious, just respectable, large and clean. John was the kind of boy that took his circumstances for granted. Frances remembered that she had noticed the fitted hall carpet first. It had muted colours and was soft underfoot. John barely looked at her, they were ushered in immediately and John's hands seemed drawn by magnetic force to Bernadette's body.

'Hang on John let's get Frances settled first.'

She was taken into a enormous sitting room where a large grey three piece seat seemed to dominate the room. There was an odd cupboard in the corner which held dainty glasses and bottles. On one shelf stood a display of glass animals she was drawn to it and stood staring at glass deer, cats and horses. Bernadette pulled her away and made her sit on the sofa; she remembered that it was so big that her legs stuck out in front of her. It was then that John gave her the biggest bar of chocolate she had ever seen.

'It's almost as big as you.' he said.

Frances liked his voice, he didn't speak like the boys on their estate. She could understand him.

'Thank you very much' she said.

'God, Bernadette your sister has an Irish accent.'

She didn't remember what Bernadette's reply was because they went upstairs to 'do art' or so they told her. She supposed she probably did have an Irish accent when she was four. She never had been to nursery and was not allowed to play with the other children on the estate. Many years later she found out that Bernadette and Maureen had been sent to elocution classes. Her sisters were made to teach Frances and Angela how to speak with English accents.

When they got home, Frances remembered feeling nervous at first, she had hated lying to her parents pretending that Bernadette had taken her to the swings. The promise that she would be given more chocolate everytime they visited John's house, made her willing to lie about anything. The next time she went it was an enormous box of Maltesers. She lost count of days and times she went, as that period of her life was just measured in chocolate.

The 'phone call had irritated her, and left her with a nagging sense of guilt. Her mother always had a knack for making her feel guilty. As usual her mother had managed to bring Bernadette into the conversation.

How she had been convinced that she had seen her yesterday. She'd tried to jolly her mother along comparing her sightings of Bernadette to those of fans of Elvis, who are convinced he is alive and well. But her mother had said that comparing Bernadette to a dead man was tactless. Tact- as if her mother knew anything about tact. The sound that tearing the chocolate wrapper made was satisfying; the smoothness of the chocolate and its familiar sweet smell was comforting. How could anything so delicious be bad for you? She suddenly had an image of the last time she made love with Dave flash into her head. She was reminded of two ridiculous Tellytubbies doing what Tellytubbies were never meant to do and she found herself laughing out loud. Sex or chocolate? No contest.

Her mother had asked her how much weight she had lost.

'Only two pounds? Well I s'pose Rome wasn't built in a day and even though you were never as pretty as the others, won't you look better once the weight is off.'

She wished she had told her mother about Bernadette at the time. There were lots of things her mother did not know about Bernadette. It was years later before Frances finally worked out what Bernadette and John were really up to, and why they had both laughed when she had asked to see John's paintings. Her parents like many immigrants had seen education as the only way that the next generation could acquire the status and wealth that they had been unable to accumulate. But, Bernadette knew that her looks and body were more of an asset than her brain and she was diligent in her pursuit of opportunities that would allow her to use her talents, in return for the best rewards.

All Frances had to show for the deception was the love of chocolate. Maureen or Christina as she prefers to be called had the looks and the brains, but a heart of ice and Angela? Earnest Angela, the baby of the family and the peacemaker. Once considered the golden girl because she had been the first person in the family to go to University and because she had married a public school boy was now turning out to be a disappointment too. Frances looked down and was surprised to see that she had just two squares of chocolate left. Chocolate bars, like wine bottles were definitely getting smaller. Those bars at John Whittaker's seemed to go on and on. She used to synchronise her chewing with the rhythm of the sounds that came from John Whittaker's bedroom.

Her mother had called to remind her that it was her 85th birthday in a few weeks time. They always tried to visit their mother on her birthday, at least Frances and Angela did. There would be hell to pay if they didn't. Ever since Bernadette had cut off all contact with them they had all had to over compensate their mother for her loss. Frances knew she was not alone in feeling relieved that Bernadette was out of their lives. Blood might be thicker than water, but she had always believed that God gave you friends to compensate for your family. She hoped that her daughter would visit her when she was older because she wanted to, not out of a sense of duty. She looked at herself in the hall mirror; but she would have to lose weight if she wanted her daughter to feel anything other than repulsion for her mother.

CHAPTER 3

Angela Everett sat alone in her breakfast room eating dry toast and listening to the Sunday service on Radio 4; it was the nearest she got to a religious experience these days. For the last eight years her Sunday mornings had been taken up by rugby. At least her son played for London Irish, whose members were predominantly Catholic, it was practically like being at Mass.

She looked at her calendar and winced-it would be Christmas before she knew it. She felt like her mother, asking herself where the year had gone. When she turned the page to check on a date, she saw a small neat entry she had made way back in January.

Mammy's 85th birthday.

Her mother said she didn't bother about her birthdays, but every year just before the end of September, she would call each daughter in turn and subtly bring the subject around to how it was 'almost October.' It had been very different when they were children. She could remember her mother saying that birthday parties were an English invention. Mammy's birthday would mean a big visit, everyone converging on what was now just Mammy's place. Angela knew she would put a lot of effort into it, but would end up feeling unappreciated. But it was one of life's duties, the sort of ritual that no one really truly enjoys but the sort that people are made better by enduring. Parenthood contained too many of these for Angela's comfort. She glanced at the clock and dragged herself out of the chair and walked to the end of the stairs.

'Fergal are you awake? You have twenty minutes to get dressed and have some breakfast, less if your kit isn't ready.'

Some hope she thought. She was about to amble back to the table when she remembered that she would have to get dressed too. The last thing she needed was to have her ex husband see her in the long white cotton night-dress and bed socks she had taken to wearing since he left home.

She opened her son's bedroom door and felt assaulted by the odour of maleness that exuded from within it. Fergal lay asleep on the bed wired up to his walkman, with the controls of his play station still in his hands. A magazine lay open at the centrefold on his floor revealing a well waxed woman. Suspicious stains on the magazine reminded Angela of the more acceptable milestones she had recorded. No wonder her mother said she was glad she never had boys. The thought of her mother being able to step over the magazine as she did now, in order to get to the window to let fresh air in amused Angela.

'Hi Mum' Fergal sat up and smiled. She could always be melted by that smile.

Angela had a quick shower and dressed in her tight-est jeans and a top that clung to her breasts. Divorce had done her figure the world of good, something that cheered her up whenever she missed having someone to mow the lawn or attend school events with. She glanced at the long case clock on the landing a wedding present to her from Mark and sighed. The inscription on its face 'Eternal love' seemed such a mockery now.

Standing in the kitchen waiting for the kettle to boil Angela's thoughts returned to her mother's birthday. She wrote herself a reminder to call Christina and Frances to discuss it with them. Only it wasn't just Mammy's birthday, it was Bernadette's too. Bernadette-her eldest sister, whom no one had seen or heard from for twenty-five years, she would be 57 now. Angela's memories of her sister were of a young glamorous woman whom she had idolised. She found it impossible to imagine what her sister would look like now. Most of the time she hardly thought about Bernadette, it was only when strangers asked her how many brothers or sisters she had that she would hesitate and face her own 'St Peter in the Garden of Gethsemane moment' should she say she had two or three sisters?

She had no time now to dwell on Bernadette; she had to cajole her son to get his act together.

'Fergal get off that play station and have some breakfast, your father will be here in five minutes. You know he gets cross if you aren't ready the moment he arrives.'

Fourteen-year-old Fergal was all that fourteen-year-old boys should be. He would be handsome again when his hormones calmed down. His Irish genes had bestowed him with dark wavy hair, creamy skin (in between the blackheads and pustules) and green-grey eyes. Angela was thankful that he had not inherited the Everett weak chin, mousy hair and piggy eyes. 'Like two burnt holes in a blanket', her mother had said when she had seen Mrs Everett for the first time at Angela and Mark's wedding.

So much had happened in the last twenty-five years that Angela wondered where Bernadette would fit in if she were to return now. They were all different people now. Her father was dead, Frances was the size of a house and the sister Bernadette knew as Maureen no longer existed, having transformed herself from a shy self conscious teenager into the cool sophisticated Christina. People expected families to be happy, sisters were meant to love each other. Angela was happy to settle for tolerance.

Mark was on time; Angela opened the door and invited him in with an easy smile and only the slight hint of awkwardness. It never failed to amaze her how civilised they were to each other now that they were divorced. Life had calmed down and settled into a pattern of access visits and discussions over where Fergal was to spend his holidays. She imagined that it wouldn't be long before Mark met someone else. The wild woman he had left her for did not stay around for long. She realised that access visits, and financing an ex wife and son meant the expensive presents, lavish meals, the weekends away she had enjoyed during the courting phase soon dried up. Angela was only a child herself. She imagined him telling her about the new woman in his life and rehearsed her reply. She hoped that he had learned from his mistakes and had made sure he found a nice Protestant English woman, from a good family.Even she would not wish his parents on anyone they did not approve of. Once after one of their many rows over his parents she had written him a reference to hand to any prospective wife. She had said that if cigarette packets have to carry health warnings so should prospective husbands. She felt any new girlfriend of Mark's would have to realise that as far as the Everett's were concerned no one would ever be suitable for their son.

Fergal thundered down the stairs to meet his father. They exchanged awkward greetings, neither wanting to show how much the other was missed. Fergal grabbed a slice of toast and followed his father out the door, remembering to say goodbye to her which was muffled on account of the toast in his mouth.

Angela waved until Mark's car was out of sight. She remembered the old days when Fergal had wanted his mother to watch him play rugby. All she had longed for was the time when she would regain her Sunday mornings. Now her whole Sunday stretched out before her and it was at times like this that she felt most lonely. However there was no space for her in Mark's car even if she wanted to go. She hoped that the new sports car he had lusted after for some time made him happy. *Dad's pulling wagon* Fergal called it. When Mark had the fling that led to the divorce, he claimed he was going through a 'mid life crisis'. Was she allowed one of those? When would she fit it in? She was always the sensible one in the family but now she just seemed to be a failure. What had she got to show for it? She was a middle aged single parent doing a dull part time job at the hospital. Her sisters were safe in their worlds, even if their worlds wouldn't be her choice.

She was sure that wherever Bernadette was she was not living a dull life. She would be living it up in some exotic part of the world still surrounded by men. Bernadette was not made for nine- to- five drudgery. She wished she could see her sister again, whenever she mentioned this to Fran and Christina they thought she was mad and said she didn't know Bernadette like they knew her. Well she was unlikely to get to know her now, but that didn't stop her wishing she could. Bernadette was always a rebel she would understand why she had not tolerated Mark's behaviour 'for the sake of your child' as her mother had said. Even Christina had spoken about 'putting up and shutting up'. Angela made herself a cup of coffee and settled down to 'phone her sisters. She glanced at the clock 9 am, too soon to ring Christina who would still be asleep, recovering from one of her and Giles' *networking* dinner parties.

'Is that Sister Frances?'

'Yes this is Sister Frances at the Convent of the devotion to chocolate.'

'It's Sister Angela from the Convent of the divorced and desperate.'

Even though both sisters were in their forties, the banter from school days stuck with them. Christina never joined in, claiming that she still had nightmares about her convent days.

'Hi Babby. Has the old gizzard picked Fergal up?'

'Yes they've just left. How's life?'

'Fabulous darling, Dave's just told me he's invited a couple he met in the pub last night for lunch and Celeste has told me she needs a mouse costume for her school play.'

'Fran you've nothing else to do with your time have you now?'

Angela as a working mother, firmly believed in the principle of if you want something doing ask a busy person.

'Here she goes, listen do you want something, is that why you're ringing me?'

'Have you remembered it's Mammy's birthday on the 15th?'

'Jesus I had, but she rang me yesterday herself and dropped lots of very unsubtle hints. It's her 85th so much for you saying she'd go quickly after Daddy.'

'Fran you're wicked, I think we should sort out a date for us all to go down to see her. It's what she'll expect. Just us girls and the kids I mean, we don't need to drag Dave and Giles down with us.'

'As long as we bring the food, you know what she's like, always trying to put me on diets.'

'Not as if you need one, is it Fran.'

'Just knowing how embarrassing it must be for you having a sister who is fat, is a great incentive to pig myself.'

'You've always been an embarrassment, even when you were stick thin.'

'Listen, do you think Christina will come?'

'You mean 'Maureen you'll always be Maureen to me' as Mammy says. Well I'm going to ask her anyway, it's about time she shared more of the burden with us.'

'Angela you're beginning to sound like Mammy, *'and after all the sacrifices I made for you'.'* You know they say you grow more like your mother the older you get.'

'Well God help us is all I can say.'

'What are we going to give her as a present?'

'Any ideas?'

'Angela you're better at that sort of thing than me. I'd buy her a big box of chocolates and then help her eat most of them.'

'Anyway I'll let you go you've got guests for lunch.'

'That! Oh I told Dave to cook it himself, he invited them.'

Angela checked her watch, 9.30am; she would email Christina and inform her of the birthday plans. Then it would then be up to her, she was not going to cajole her.

Christina had replied by late afternoon, no doubt after she had woken up, eaten a leisurely breakfast and read the papers. Angela sometimes felt envious of her sister's lifestyle. Christina was a good advert for being childless, she looked much younger than 52 with the time and money to indulge herself in regular facials and trips to the health spa. Angela had wanted wanted a different life a wedding, a husband and children. She had just wanted to be like everyone else.

Christina's reply was short and to the point, 'I'll be

there, she won't live forever. If you buy the present I will contribute £10.'

Angela had stripped the beds done several loads of washing and had cleaned the house by the time she received Christina's reply. She would sit down and think about a suitable present for their mother, which both Frances and Christina assumed she would buy, once she had sorted Fergal's uniform and packed his sports bag.